THE SISTER PACT

HOME IS WHERE THE HEART IS

JACQUIE BIGGAR

WAVEFRONT PUBLISHING

PRAISE FOR JACQUIE BIGGAR

My Girl

My Girl has everything to love in a novel: hunky and handsome cowboys with soft hearts, second chance romances, cute kids and some secrets and suspense thrown in.

— *COLORADO COWGIRL*

Skating on Thin Ice

Jacquie Biggar has done it again. I have yet another new book boyfriend—Mac Wanowski, captain of the Victoria WarHawks hockey team.

— WRITESTER

The Lady Said No

*"The Lady Said No is an **addictive mystery** filled with **cagy characters** with the backdrop of the greatest horse race known to man."*

— AMAZON REVIEWER

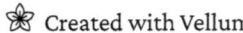 Created with Vellum

For my extended Family, The Authors' Billboard

Without the friendship of these ladies, I don't know where I would be. They spur me on to be a better writer, support each other in times of distress, and cheer our successes. Many thanks to Mimi Barbour for seeing something in me that I didn't know I had, and to everyone in the group for their love and kindness.

Jacquie

Sister is probably the most competitive relationship within the family, but once the sisters are grown, it becomes the strongest relationship.

— MARGARET MEAD

INTRODUCTION

"What are you thinking?" Levi asked, lips lifting in that familiar quirk that managed to do odd things to her pulse.

"How surprised I am that we got through the day without a single argument," she taunted, with a grin of her own.

He reached out and grasped her hand resting on the seat between them. "I'm glad you agreed to come out with me," he said, his thumb caressing her palm.

She shifted until he released his hold, heat rising to her cheeks. "I am, too. I have to admit I didn't know what to expect."

He eyed her quizzically. "Did you think I planned to have my nefarious way with you?"

She laughed, but her girl bits quivered at the thought. "Don't be silly, I'm hardly your type." Levi pulled into her parents' driveway and parked. Holly fidgeted under his steady regard. "What?" She rubbed at an imaginary speck on her cheek. "Do I have dirt on my face?"

She stilled as he reached out and brushed a stray lock of hair behind her ear. His knuckles grazing her skin sent involuntary shivers chasing each other up her spine. His eyes had darkened, the humor replaced by something she feared putting a name to. He couldn't be attracted to her; could he?

"Levi..."

"Shh," he murmured, leaning until their lips were a breath apart. "You have the most delectable lips. I've been wanting to kiss them all day." He turned his hand to cup her jaw. "What do you say, Holly Anderson? Will you let me? I wonder."

He didn't wait for a reply. His mouth eased over hers and it sent common sense flying out the window. He didn't rush, instead taking time to taste her as though she mattered to him. It was slow and sensuous, and she never wanted it to end. She moaned, helpless to hide the yearning he'd brought barreling to life. She touched her tongue to his, then withdrew, made vulnerable by the sensations coursing through her body.

"Levi," she said again, though she wasn't sure what she was asking anymore.

He moved his hand to her nape and tugged,

drawing her into his seductive web and she was help-less to escape. Didn't want to, even if she could.

"I've imagined this moment for so many years," he rasped, shocking her to the core.

How could that be? They barely knew one another. His kisses were like a drug, making it hard to think. There was something she should clarify, but...

A horn blared behind them. Holly jumped like a scalded cat, while Levi slowly, ever so slowly, eased back to his side of the vehicle. He started the engine and lowered the steamy windows, letting fresh air flow in along with awareness. They were making out on a public street like two teenagers in the throes of passion. What was she thinking? She hadn't been, that was the problem. An affair with Levi would never work. There was far too much water under the bridge between their families and her own drunken mistake ten years ago. In all reality, she was surprised he wanted anything to do with her.

"Umm, that was unexpected," she said, for lack of brilliant repartee. Her brain cells were still playing catch up with her hormones.

CHAPTER
ONE

Holly Tremaine glared after the cabbie who'd just driven away with her carefully wrapped Christmas gifts in the backseat. She'd done everything short of flying to catch his attention, all to no avail. Now what was she going to do? She hadn't even caught the number of his taxi. The car was blue and white, and the cab driver had been an older man with pictures of his two grandchildren taped to his dash—that's all the information she had.

What a mess.

The bluebird of lost hopes—aka the cab—disappeared into the busy Victoria traffic leaving Holly alone to face her past. She swallowed hard and turned toward her parents' imposing two-story townhouse. The dismal day blended with the gray stone and black iron accents that had intimidated her as a child—nice to see some things remained the same.

Sighing, she tightened her grip on the carry-on bag she'd limited herself to for the flight—which is why she was now giftless—and trudged toward the big oak doors as though she were fighting her way through quicksand. Great. Not even in the house and she already regretted the trip.

The sign below the bell was no less glaring for the elegant script; No Soliciting, Fundraising, Salesmen, Religion or Politics- Thank you.

As though attaching manners at the end softened the cold tone the message conveyed. That was her parents in a nutshell.

She jabbed the bell like it was a release valve for her frustration. The rain that had held off while she dashed from store to store began to fall—a misty drizzle that sank into Holly's clothes and turned her hair lank in a matter of seconds. Wet and miserable, she waited for someone to let her in.

The door swung back revealing a yawning black maw—or so it seemed in that moment. The one person Holly had hoped to avoid stood in the entry.

Her sister.

"Holly." Susan looked down her slender, too perfect, nose. "You're late."

Holly blew a wayward strand of wet hair away from her face and tried to ignore the tic developing over her right eyebrow. "Well, I'm here now. Better late than never, right?" She glanced over her shoulder at the curtain of rain. "Mind letting me in? It's cold out here." She smiled and took a step forward, forcing her sister to move or get plowed down.

The grand entrance was just as inhospitable as she remembered. Dark wood climbed the walls while marble tile covered the floor like a layer of ice. Eight years and nothing had changed.

"Where are they?" she asked, though she knew the answer by glancing at her watch. Five o'clock, time for pre-dinner drinks in the lounge.

"Mom and Dad? Or Steven?"

The nervous tap-tapping of Susan's glossy black pump told Holly she wasn't nearly as calm as she pretended. For her part, Holly couldn't control the fluttering in her stomach at the thought of seeing Steven after all these years. Her sister looked... older —harder. Maybe married life hadn't turned out like she expected. Was it wrong Holly hoped that was true?

"I just arrived, Sue." They'd both used nicknames for each other as children. "Can we save the arguing until tomorrow? I'm beat."

Susan's expression softened as though she, too, regretted the distance that had grown between them. "Hols, we need to..."

"Who was at the door, darling? Your parents are

acting even stranger than normal." Steven approached from down the hall, his view obstructed by his wife.

Breathe, Holly. She was going to hyperventilate and embarrass herself by passing out on the floor at their feet, she could see it now. Well, she could if not for the black dots dancing before her eyes. *Oh man*, he was every bit as striking as she remembered. Movie star handsome. And at one time, the love of her life. No matter how many pep-talks she'd given herself, nothing could have prepared her for this.

Her vision blurred. She leaned hard on the handle of her luggage as her knees wobbled, then gasped as the wheels slipped out from under her and she went down, landing hard on her elbow.

"Ow," she muttered, almost as an afterthought, too busy trying to control her flip-flopping tummy. "I don't feel so good." At least the tiles were cool on her back—small favors.

"Take it easy," a rich, deep voice murmured. And then he was there. Warm hands cradled her head while wide shoulders blocked the vision of Susan's surprisingly worried expression. Strange, she thought Susan would be laughing at her predicament.

"I'm fine," she snapped, wriggling to escape Steven's hold. But then she looked into his eyes and froze. Steven's eyes were the blue of a midnight sky. These eyes matched the winter storm lashing the window panes—grim and steely. "You," she whispered, stunned.

"Were you hoping for someone else?" Steven's annoying, pain-in-her-butt brother asked.

Holly lay back and closed her eyes. "Why can't I catch a break?"

CHAPTER
TWO

Levi Anderson stared down at his sister-in-law's gamine face with its pale cheeks and distracting pink lips. The last time he'd had his hands on Holly was at his twin brother's wedding fiasco eight years ago. He was dismayed to find the attraction hadn't faded. It had been a mistake then, and it was a mistake now.

"C'mon princess, time to quit faking a faint." *Three, two...*

Her green-gold eyes popped open on an indignant huff. "I'm *not* faking, you, you... oaf." She shoved his hand away, blinking as her head hit the floor. "Let me up."

He stood, happy to put some space between them. "Sure. It's just like you to make an entrance." Not true.

Melodrama was much more Susan's forte. "Here," he held out his hand, "grab hold."

She looked like she'd sooner crawl down the hall than accept his help, but common sense won out. Even though her fingers were chilled from being outdoors, she still struck sparks off his skin. She came up in a rush, her head no more than chest-high. He'd forgotten how small she was—delicate.

"Thanks," she muttered, yanking her hand back to brush the damp skirt down her thighs.

"If we're done with the histrionics, Mother and Daddy are waiting," Susan said, her gaze impatient.

Levi ignored her. "You okay now?" he asked Holly. She was still far too pallid for his liking.

She nodded, shivering slightly in her damp clothing. "It's been a long day and I forgot to eat, that's all." She turned to her sister. "Are Amy and Jacob here?"

Susan led the way toward the lounge. "They're home with a sitter. I thought it best for tonight's visit."

The undercurrents between those two were thick enough to choke a horse. Levi had wondered over the years why Holly never came home, but guilt and life kept him from enquiring too deeply—now he wished he had.

Holly hesitated in the doorway as though unsure of her welcome. Her parents sat separately—one on the settee, the other in a deep club chair—and remained sitting, just another night at the Tremaine home.

Steven set a drink—his third in an hour—on the fireplace mantle, ignored his father-in-law's disapproving glare, and strode across the room to hug Holly, wrapping her in a bruising hold.

"Welcome home, Holly Berry. It's been too long." He planted a lingering kiss on her cheek before grasping her hands and raising them to his lips. "I've missed you." Susan snorted and he let Holly go to wrap an arm around his wife's waist, squeezing her against his side. "We all have."

Levi decided to step in before his idiot brother got himself into even more trouble than he was already in. He placed a guiding hand on Holly's lower back and led her forward. "Why don't you say hello to your parents, I'll get you a drink."

He could practically feel each bone of her vertebrae snap to attention the closer they got to the elder Tremaines. For her sake he willed them to rise and properly greet their daughter, but it wasn't to be. Instead, her mother turned her cheek for a light peck and her father raised his glass in a toast.

"Welcome home to the prodigal child. We were beginning to wonder if the next time we saw you would be graveside."

"Daddy," Susan hissed. "Don't say such things. You

know how upset Mother gets when you talk about death."

"Ha." He laughed. "She's had my burial suit washed and pressed for months now."

Not to be outdone, Mrs. Tremaine eyed her husband's glass. "Just keep drinking, George, and my fondest wish will come true."

Holly sank onto the far end of the sofa as though her legs wouldn't carry her any farther. "I see not much has changed," she said, peeling the wet jacket down her arms. "You and Father have been trying to kill each other off since we were children." She shared a glance with her sister. "I'm glad no one succeeded."

"Why would you care?" her mother said, chin in the air. "You went off to the big city and forgot all about your family."

"Momma, that's not true," Holly protested. "You know it was always my dream to attend Juilliard."

Her father snorted into his drink. "No matter the cost."

Levi set the bottle of rum on the bar with a thunk. He couldn't believe what he was hearing. Claire and George were punishing their daughter for chasing her destiny. He'd always found them to be cordial, if somewhat standoffish. He never would have guessed they could be so cold to their own offspring.

He traded a glance with Steven—who did little

more than shrug—before carrying the rum and ginger drink to Holly.

"Drink this, it'll warm you up."

She eyed him doubtfully but took a careful sip. And choked. Levi sank down beside her, removed the glass from her grip before she spilled it, and gave her back a couple of solid whoomphs.

Tears sprang from the corner of her eyes. She coughed a few more times before leaning away from him. "What are you trying to do, kill me?"

He grinned. At least she had some color now. "It's my version of a rum toddy, guaranteed to fix what ails you."

"*You* are what ails me," she sputtered.

"Leave the poor girl alone before you scare her back to the Big Apple," Steven said from his position on the arm of Susan's chair, one leg dangling like a pendulum. "Though, who could blame her?"

"I'm not going home until after the holidays." Holly looked at her sister. "We have lost time to make up."

Anger, and something like pain, flashed in Susan's eyes before she brought it under control, her expression as smooth as the Juan de Fuca Strait at dusk. Placid.

But Levi was well aware of the danger lying below the surface.

H olly tried to pay attention to the sporadic conversation at the dinner table without being viscerally aware of the man seated to her right, but it was a lost cause. Levi took up all the space between them even though he was careful to keep his elbows in while eating the herb and garlic stuffed lamb tenderloin, roasted vegetables and mashed potato cakes.

"Pass the asparagus," her father said from his position at the head of the table. Holly handed the platter of steaming vegetables with capers and roasted nuts to Levi who passed it down the way.

He had a sort of effortless charisma, she decided. The overhead lights picked up the walnut tones in his slightly wavy hair. He'd rolled the sleeves on his light blue dress shirt leaving strong, tanned forearms with a smattering of golden-brown hair that distracted her when he moved. Then there was his scent—a subtle mixture of fresh cut wood and spice that drew her closer even as she leaned away.

"What are you doing here, Levi?" she murmured. "I wouldn't have figured you for a family gathering."

He handed her a plate of flaky dinner rolls. "Are you kidding? With free food and entertainment, how could I say no?"

"Always the comedian, aren't you?" she retorted, ripping a bun in half.

"What are you two whispering about?" Susan stared from across the table with suspicious eyes.

Steven waved a forkful of lamb in their direction. "There are no secrets allowed in this household, ask my darling wife."

Susan scowled, her contempt obvious. "You're drunk."

"Can we have just one meal together without it becoming a slinging match?" Claire said, tossing her spotless linen napkin beside her plate. She wrapped talon-like fingers around the stem of her wine glass and took a long drink before setting it down with careful precision.

"Where's the fun in that?" Steven said under his breath.

Holly had the insane desire to laugh. As dysfunctional as her family was, they were never boring. "I've missed you all," she said. "I wish you could have come to New York to see me play the violin." *On my first opening night.*

"But—" Steven started.

"Dinner is delicious, Claire," Levi cut in. "My regards to the chef."

Claire's cheeks flushed. "Thank you, my dear. At least someone appreciates my efforts." She slid a sideways glower toward her husband.

"Would it really matter if I gave you a compliment?" he said, calmly taking a bite of his asparagus. "You quit caring what I thought long ago."

"Daddy," Susan gasped, and Holly was surprised to see tears glittering in her sister's cornflower blue eyes. "How could you?"

"Enough. We have guests," Claire bit off through pinched lips. She picked up the napkin and dabbed her brow, then lifted her chin and smiled at Levi. "Why don't you tell Holly what you've been up to the past few years—I'm sure she'd love to hear about it. After all, you have a lot in common."

Holly's gaze ping-ponged from her sister to her parents, and finally landed on Levi's too-handsome face. The empathy tingeing his expression only ramped up her concern. Her parents had a love-hate relationship, but she'd never heard them speak so bitterly. Were they easing toward a divorce?

"Levi is in the music business, too. Personally, I

think he does it for the chicks, right bro?" Steven gave his brother an exaggerated wink.

Levi frowned. "Time to switch to water, *bro*." He turned to Holly. "I started a small music agent company a few years ago and it's done relatively well. Nothing like your career, though." He gazed at her with an admiration that made her ears grow hot.

She didn't know what to do with this version of Levi. Other than their one monumental mistake of a night together, they'd given each other a wide berth the few times Steven had brought them together.

Steven.

Holly peeked at him from under her lashes. He looked unhappy—older. Instead of the satisfaction she expected to feel, there was only melancholy. Her family was in turmoil and she'd had no idea.

"You sell yourself short, Levi." Susan raised a well-defined brow at Holly, letting her know she'd been caught staring at her sister's husband. "Your business is listed as one of Canada's top fifty up and coming companies to watch. Quite the accomplishment, I'd say."

"Maybe you married the wrong brother," Steven muttered.

"How are the children?" Holly asked, desperate to end the bickering. Her head pounded from the tension pervading the room. She'd flown in for each of their births, video messaged them on their birthdays and sent fabulous auntie presents but had failed miserably in the hugs department. She hoped to change that in the future, starting with Christmas.

Susan smiled, a mother's love and pride softening her porcelain perfection. "They're growing so fast I can barely keep up. Jacob is in grade three French immersion. His teacher declares he's smart as a whip and rarely gets into mischief. Amy, on the other hand —" She shared an intimate look with Steven, and he laced their fingers together. "Let's just say she keeps us on our toes and leave it at that." She lifted their bound fingers and kissed the back of his hand.

Finally, a crack in her sister's armor. Relief loosened the pressure in Holly's skull. Maybe it wasn't too late. When she'd made the split-second decision to leave New York, she'd done so under a wave of uncertainty. Her life was good. Coming home, that was the unknown. She prayed it wasn't a mistake.

LEVI SIGHED when the meal ended without any lasting damage. He'd known when Steven invited him over from Vancouver that his brother was nervous about Holly's return. Judging by Susan's animosity, he'd been right to worry. Then again, if she hadn't slept with her sister's boyfriend and gotten pregnant, none of this would have happened.

Holly had put on a brave front, but he could see she was deflating the longer the evening dragged on. Time to wrap things up.

He leaned back in his chair and stretched, faking a yawn. "Sorry about that, it's been a long day." He nodded to his hosts. "Thanks for a lovely meal, George. Claire. You spoil me every time I visit." He turned to Steven. "Call me in the morning before my flight." He waited until his brother acknowledged the direct order, then rose. "Holly, walk me to the door?"

She froze, the water glass halfway to her lips. "Umm, sure." She carefully set the glass down and smiled uncertainly at her family before rising to join him. "I'll just be a moment," she said, as though offering an apology.

Damn it. She needed to grow a backbone around this pack of hyenas—they'd happily gnaw on her carcass if she wasn't careful.

He waited until they were out of earshot before grasping her arm to slow the race to the door. Good to know she was as uncomfortable around him as he felt with her.

"Hang on a minute, I have a couple of things to say," he murmured, surprised by the delicacy of her frame. "Are you sick?" he asked abruptly, then could have kicked his own ass for uttering the words.

She gasped and flung back her head, pride stamped all over her fine features. "That's not something you ask a lady," she snapped and wriggled free of his hold. "Just because we...," she flushed, "were close one night, it doesn't give you the right to stick your nose into my affairs."

Levi was ashamed to admit there wasn't a lot about the night of his brother's wedding that he remembered other than an unexpectedly passionate encounter with the woman in front of him. The solemn bridesmaid had come apart in his arms with an abandon he never would have expected.

He'd known she was heartbroken over Steven and Susan's betrayal, but had handled it with a quiet dignity that tugged at his heart. She'd done her best to cover her hurt in front of the family and guests, but he could see how much it cost her and it pissed him off. Steven may be his twin, but that's where it ended. They were as different as it was possible to be.

Steven was a player—he always had been—and Levi had given in to his pranks because it was easier than putting up with his brother's volatile temper. There were times they'd taken each other's classes, pulled tricks on their friends, even switched dates. He'd been sure they would get called out considering their personalities were as different as night and day, but no one seemed to notice. Like Holly with her sister, he'd often been passed over for Steven's more flamboyant behavior—which was fine by him.

Until Steven met Holly in their last year of high school.

Levi had hated the instantaneous attraction he'd felt for Holly himself. He started avoiding his brother, skipping classes and staying out late—all to avoid the dreaded *talks* Steven liked to have about his girlfriends. Levi didn't want to know how long it took him to get into her pants. His brother kept a running count of his conquests, like they were badges for his wall or something. Then Susan set her sights on Steven and the rest, as they say, was history.

"You're right, I apologize," he said. "It's just that you seem tired and I was... concerned."

She brushed wavy hair behind her shell-like ear with its tiny pearl studs and shrugged. "I'm fine. It was a long flight. I'll be right as rain tomorrow."

What was the matter with him? Obviously, she didn't want anything to do with him. He should just go. "Okay, well, I'll be heading home tomorrow—Vancouver—so I probably won't see you again before you leave. Take care of yourself." He awkwardly patted her shoulder, all the while calling himself an idiot. They were never a thing, of course she was anxious to be rid of him.

"Oh," she said, sounding bereft. "I... I thought you were staying for the holidays as well. For the children," she hurried to add.

He stared into her eyes and saw her dread. What

the hell? He had the distinct feeling she wanted him to stay. And like a fool, his heart listened.

Before he could change his mind, he let the words tumble. "Once again, you're right. I can hold off my business a couple of weeks—for the children."

Her smile and how it sent a warm glow sweeping through his chest was a warning he chose to ignore.

Holly woke the next morning in her childhood bedroom, though it looked nothing like it had when she was growing up. Her pretty white princess bed with its matching night table and dresser had been upgraded to a queen-size suite that was comfortable but hardly sentimental. The trophies and ribbons she'd won in school for music competitions were gone. Even the family photos she'd hung on the taupe walls had disappeared.

As though she'd been erased.

Maybe that wasn't so far from the truth. Ever since she'd contracted Lyme disease, her life had unspooled. The diagnosis and treatment were bad enough, but the debilitating weakness and fatigue, the headaches, fevers and chills robbed Holly of the ability to perform up to the standard her tour company rightfully expected, and she'd been forced to take an extended leave of absence. Her friends, while sympathetic, had full lives of their own and rarely managed to stop by for visits. Lonely and depressed, the time during convalescence forced Holly to rethink her priorities. If her family wouldn't come to her, then she'd go to them.

Except it seemed as though they'd managed just fine without her.

Enough with the self-pity party already.

She threw back the covers and rose, pleased to find the aches and pains of the day before had all but disappeared. The doctors had warned her not to overdo things and get plenty of rest. Yesterday was a brutal reminder of what could happen if she ignored their advice. She checked the time on her cellphone and gasped—ten o'clock? Why didn't anyone wake her up? She wasn't here to sleep the entire holiday away.

A quick shower and change of clothes later, Holly opened her bedroom door and hurried down the stairs leading into the kitchen at the rear of the house. She slowed when her mother's disembodied voice floated into the stairwell.

"I don't care what you think, that girl is hiding something."

"If she is, she'll tell us when she's ready. Leave the child alone, Claire." Her father sounded irritated.

It wasn't a secret. Holly wanted to inform them of her illness in person, that's all. She hadn't meant to cause more dissension.

"That's your answer to everything, George. Stick your head in the sand and pretend nothing is wrong."

A plate crashed into the sink.

Holly gasped and covered her mouth. Should she retreat to her room? This was a private argument. Her parents would be upset to learn it had been overheard. She turned to climb the stairs and slipped. Her elbow banged the brass railing, and like a gong, her resultant cry announced her arrival. There was no hiding now.

She pasted a smile on frozen lips and stiffly descended into the war-zone. The air vibrated with tension. Her mother stood at the far end of the kitchen, arms wrapped tightly around a still-trim body —a barren island in the sunlit room.

Her father was at the sink, gingerly reaching for the shards of china—broken, like their marriage.

Holly didn't know what to do, what to say, so she remained still, that *stupid* smile glued to her lips.

"I suppose you heard everything?" her mother accused, eyes snapping.

"Claire—" her dad muttered. "For Pete's sake, have some pride."

"Pride. That's rich coming from you," she spat.

"Umm, good morning?" Holly stammered, her heart beating like a mad thing. She put a hand to her

chest as though she could trap it in place. "I slept in."
Too bad it wasn't for longer.

Her father was the first to move. He crossed the room to plant a dry kiss on Holly's cheek. "Good morning, pumpkin. Did you get a good rest?"

Ookay, then. Obviously, they were going to play the ignore-the-elephant-in-the-room game. She nodded. "Yes, thank you. The bed was nice."

"I suppose we should have warned you," her mother said, striding to the cupboard to remove a coffee cup. "We updated your bedroom a couple of years after you... left. Coffee?"

Holly grimaced. "I didn't *leave*, Mom. I went to school. It's not the end of the world, you know. Lot's of kids do it." She accepted the steaming coffee cup. "Thanks."

"You're welcome. Your father and I were just about to leave. We have an appointment downtown—shouldn't be long. Will you be all right here?"

Well, I won't burn the place down, if that's what you're getting at. "Sure. Maybe I'll see what Susan is doing. I'd love to visit with the children."

"Holly, really. They're in school. Are you that out of touch you don't know your own niece and nephew's schedule?" Her mother tut-tutted and slid a piece of pink notepaper with elegant handwriting across the counter. "Here's our cell numbers and your sister's—in case you don't remember them."

The snide reference didn't go unnoticed. Holly's father's forehead curdled, matching the sour expression marring his handsome face. "Is it any wonder she moved away?" He snagged his keys from the counter and stomped out the door, disgusted.

Holly's mom, on the other hand, took her time. She cleaned the broken plate from the sink, tossing it into the trash as though it wasn't one of her favorite china dishes, put away the odds and ends from breakfast, then slid into a navy-blue raincoat before turning toward the door—all the while avoiding eye contact with Holly. "There's a plate in the refrigerator if you're hungry. You look tired, you should rest." She was about to disappear out the door when she glanced over her shoulder. "I'm glad you're home," she said and then she was gone on a breath of Chanel.

Tears sprang to Holly's eyes. Maybe it wasn't too late after all.

CHAPTER
FIVE

Susan rushed around her spacious contemporary kitchen—Steven's choice—slapping together lunches; ham and cheese sandwiches, grape and strawberry fruit snacks, along with a chocolate milk for Jacob and apple juice for Amy. Next, she prepared Steven's coffee and morning breakfast of two boiled eggs with multigrain toast, his tablet at the ready to read the latest news.

"Hurry up, kids, or you'll be late for school." Amy had milk from her cereal dripping down her chin and Jacob was still in pyjamas. Susan sighed, tired already and the day had just begun. She wet a sheet of paper towelling, gently cleaned her daughter's rosy face and kissed her forehead. "Jacob, I need you to walk your sister into class today, okay?"

"But, Mom..." he complained just as Steven

entered the kitchen, briefcase in one hand while the other straightened his tie.

"Do as your mother tells you, Jake," he warned, scooping up his tablet and adding it to the outside pocket of his case.

Susan frowned. "I made breakfast." She was whining but dammit, couldn't he take five minutes to spend with his kids before rushing out the door?

He barely glanced at the place setting, that silly curl of golden-brown hair flirting with his brow. "Sorry, babe, gotta fly. Big account in the works and if I'm late…"

What? The sky will fall? Churlish thoughts roiled in her brain, but she held it all in—the ever-dutiful wife. "Aren't you going to ask why I can't take Amy to class?"

He smiled at her as though humoring the baby. "Sure. What's so important you can't take our daughter to school today?"

I'm going to be busy screwing the mailman, hovered on the tip of her tongue, but big ears were listening. "Five minutes, Jacob. Go get dressed. Now."

The mom voice did its job. Amy, ever her brother's shadow, hopped down and followed Jacob from the room.

Like I was with Holly.

Regret was a bitter pill to swallow—Lord knows, she'd downed enough of them. But she'd won, right?

The handsome husband, showy house, expensive cars, beautiful children—so why did she feel so empty inside?

"I'm going to see Holly," she stated abruptly, taking in Steven's startled expression with cynicism. "Is that a problem?"

He played with the locks on his briefcase. *Snap. Snap.* "Of course not. I'm sure you two will have lots to catch up on."

You have no idea.

"Eight years is a long time." She waited but of course he played the innocent, stepping close to peck her cheek.

"Okay, well, enjoy your visit. I might be late tonight—the case, you know. Give Holly a hug for me. She looks good, doesn't she? That frail vibe must have the guys lining up to be her hero." He grinned engagingly and snatched the Porsche keys off the hook on his way out the door.

Unlike me, you mean. Susan was well aware she fell short in the damsel in distress category. She'd outgrown her sister by a foot in seventh grade, and while it was gratifying to be the tall blonde with a runway figure back then, now she just wished Steven looked at her like he did her sister.

She picked up his untouched breakfast and crossed to the sink. While the garbage disposal did its job, she stared out the window, willing Steven to look her way as he exited the family's three-car garage, but of course he didn't. She could see him talking via hands-free and wondered who it was as he wheeled his showy car onto the street and roared away with a squeal of tires. Maybe she didn't want to know.

Maybe if she ignored the signs, they would disappear. She'd told herself for months now that it was her imagination; Steven would never leave her and the children.

Nothing said he couldn't be having an affair though.

After all, he'd done it before—with her.

Ironic, really.

"Mommy, I said we're ready."

Amy's shrill little voice broke through Susan's painful reflections. She turned to her children with a relieved smile, "Okay then, race you to the car."

Amy squealed and took off, pigtails bouncing as she skipped from the room. Jacob hesitated, his solemn gaze worried.

"Are you sad, Mom? Dad didn't mean to miss breakfast."

Her big boy. He sensed trouble, though not the reason behind it. Pray he never found out. She tousled his corn silk hair—so like his father's—and tapped him lightly on his freckled nose. "How did you get to be so smart?" He blushed and her heart clenched. He was growing up too fast. It wouldn't be long before there were spring dances, girls calling, driving and college; she just hoped Steven would be there to help guide him into adulthood.

"Better hurry or your sister will never let you live it down." She gave him a quick hug, inhaling his little boy scent—bubblegum toothpaste—and turned away on the pretext of getting her purse before he saw her tears.

Damn Steven.

Levi parked in front of his brother's law firm and contemplated the wisdom of cornering him in his den. It had to be done. As usual, Steven was flirting with danger, only this time he'd be lucky if it didn't bite him in the ass.

The business took up the main floor of a colorful Victorian two-story home situated in scenic James Bay. Family law must pay well. The sky was an impossible blue today, so vivid he was tempted to let sleeping dogs lie and spend the afternoon at Beacon Hill Park instead of the confrontation barreling his way.

A woman towing a young boy by the hand as she left the office with tear-bright eyes steeled his resolve. That could be Susan and his nephew if he didn't step up and straighten his twin out before it was too late.

A horse-drawn carriage rounded the corner with a stream of traffic trailing behind like colorful banners. The white steed wore heavy black harnesses decorated with gleaming silver accents while the carriage itself was festooned in an array of flowers and ribbons. The happy couple sitting in the back, snuggled in a cozy blanket, were too wrapped up in each other to mind the noisy traffic or cool December temperatures. Briefly, Levi imagined himself and Holly under those covers and his blood heated. She was the most annoying woman on the face of the planet—always had been—but there was no denying the chemistry between them. Steven had his chance; he'd let her go. Levi didn't plan on making the same mistake.

The bell above the door dinged as he entered, alerting the middle-aged woman sitting behind the receptionist's desk.

"Hello, may I... Oh," she said, looking up with a social smile that morphed into the real thing. "Levi, what a nice surprise. Your brother didn't mention you were in town."

Levi grinned and accepted an enveloping hug. "It was last minute, a surprise visit. Is he in?"

She patted his arm and took a step back. "Yes, but fair warning, he's something of a bear this morning— you didn't hear that from me," she added with a wink.

"When are you going to ditch this guy and come work for me, Peggy? He doesn't deserve you." Levi said, only half kidding. Peggy was a treasure. She ran a tight ship. Steven was lucky to have her.

She chuckled. "Flattery will get you everywhere, young man." She sidled to her side of the desk and checked the computer. "Steven has another appointment in twenty minutes. Does that give you enough time?"

"That's perfect," he said. "You're a doll. I'll let myself in. Don't forget my offer, it's always open." He smiled and headed toward one of the closed office doors. *Steven Anderson; Family Lawyer & Mediator* etched on a brass plaque directed him to door number three. He gave the frosted glass a light tap and entered at the same time, catching an annoyed glare before his brother had time to cover it up.

"Levi, I wasn't expecting you." Steven rose, his high-end suit pants holding their crease, and circled a black monstrosity of a desk to grip his hand. "How did you find the office? We just moved here a few months ago."

Levi shook his hand, absently noticing the difference between his own calloused fingers and Steven's manicured skin. But then, it was all about the image with him—always had been. He held up his cell phone. "You can find anything with these things." He took a seat on one of two plush armchairs that weren't nearly as comfortable as they looked. "So, what's with the new digs? Quite the commute from Bear Mountain. Must cut into family time."

Steven stiffened, obviously not happy with where this little convo was heading. *Too damn bad.*

"Susan understands," he said, striding to a side-table loaded with a range of expensive bottles of alcohol. He unscrewed the top from a cut glass decanter. The whiskey had an amber glint under the light streaming in through a beveled glass window with a jaw-dropping view of the ocean and mountains beyond.

Levi glanced at the utilitarian watch on his wrist—a gift from their father. "Kind of early, isn't it?" He worried about his brother's drinking. It seemed to be getting worse instead of better and was just another reason he needed to get to the bottom of whatever was going on with him.

"What, are you my keeper now?" Steven's eyes narrowed. He tipped the glass back, swallowing half of his drink in one gulp—without choking.

Levi shook his head. "Drink yourself into an early grave, if you want, but you might give a little consideration to your children. They want their father back." Steven's knuckles turned white where he gripped the glass and Levi braced, prepared to duck if it came flying at him. If there was one thing he'd learned in thirty years, it was how to get under his brother's skin.

Instead of making good use of his high school

championship pitching arm, Steven refilled his glass and slunk around the desk to slouch into his leather chair. He swiveled toward the window and stared into space. "Do you think I made a mistake?" He shot a quick, over-the-shoulder glance at Levi before returning to his contemplation of the sky. "I mean this building is perfectly situated in the heart of the downtown core, but the cost... it's taking everything I have to stay afloat."

Levi released a silent sigh of relief. When Steven mentioned a mistake, his thoughts immediately jumped to Holly. If the cause of his brother's discontent was business related, it was fixable. Much easier than broken marriage vows.

He took a better look at the room they were in. It boasted mile-high ceilings with timber beams, a working—by the look of it—fireplace with a brick façade, and worn, but beautiful hardwood flooring. In other words, the office reeked of class. Perfect for a lawyer.

"Have you voiced your concerns to your wife?" If she was a part of the decision-making process, chances were she wouldn't feel quite so left out.

Steven swung around and smacked his glass onto the desk with a dull thud. "You're kidding, right? Susan doesn't care about my career. As long as the money rolls in, she's wife of the year."

Levi frowned. That didn't sound like a happily

married man. "Are you sure you're not foisting some of your own dissatisfaction onto her? From what I've seen of Susan, she's a hundred and ten percent in your court. Maybe you need to give her a chance."

"And maybe you need to mind your own business, brother." Steven stood and leaned over the desk, hands flattened on the lacquered surface. "What are you doing here, Levi? I expected you to be wooing the fair Holly after your performance last night."

Levi gritted his teeth. "What is that supposed to mean? I helped your wife's sister when she fainted. It's what any good Samaritan would do—get your dirty mind out of the gutter. Just because we share the same blood, doesn't mean we think the same way... *brother*."

Steven smirked and dropped into his chair. If he had a moustache, Levi bet he'd be twisting the ends right now. *Shit*, he'd given himself away. Steven knew how to read him better than anyone, even their parents. Everyone thought having a twin was remarkable; someone who looked like you, thought like you, combined birthdays and mannerisms, but there were just as many downsides to sharing a zygote with a sibling. Loss of individuality, privacy and maybe most of all—love. He'd lost Holly to his brother once, he didn't plan on letting it happen again.

CHAPTER

SIX

L eft on her own, Holly roamed from room to room in the stylish townhome. Everything from the hardwood flooring to the wainscoting and artistic lighting was impeccably melded to showroom quality—not a coaster or pillow out of place. She tipped a moody-looking print by famed British Columbian artist and author, Emily Carr, just to see how long it took for their parents to notice. Who was she kidding? Her mom would see it the moment she walked through the door.

The perfect precision of the home was an echo of the stiffness between her parents. They'd never been exuberant with their affections, but this was different. Cold. Clinical.

Holly felt as though she was wandering through an alternate universe. One filled by betrayal and divorce. While she'd been pursuing a career, her family had imploded. And the worst part; no one had thought to call her. Over-sensitive or not, it felt like she'd been disowned, and it hurt.

At the end of the hall, she pressed a hand against the door to her father's sanctuary—his office. Many evenings she and Susan would sit at his feet and listen enthralled while he regaled them with tales of pirates and princesses, mischievous elves and buried treasure. As with every good fairytale, a dashing hero would arrive just in time to save the day. It was probably then, listening to stories at her father's knee, that Holly began to dream of her own hero. He'd need to be strong enough to slay dragons. Charming and kind, yet able to make her laugh. Handsome and gentle; a father as perfect as her own. A good kisser; that's as far as her nine-year-old mind would go at the time. And above all else, someone she could talk to, share ideas with.

Even then, she'd known the value of a true friend.

The rattle of a key in the front door lock jerked her back to the moment. Self-conscious, she dropped her hand from where it had been resting and turned to greet her parents.

Except it wasn't her mother and father.

Susan hesitated on the threshold, their gazes fusing across the distance. A cold draft knifed its way between them filled with ugly words and betrayals.

Holly was the first to break free. She waded through the debris of the past, a plastic smile on her lips and went to meet her sister. "Great minds think alike. I'd planned on stopping by your house this morning until Mother informed me you have a life."

Something cynical flashed in Susan's blue eyes before she stepped in and closed the door, sucking the fresh air out of the entry. "She called and *suggested* I get over here and straighten out our differences." She held her hands out in mock supplication. "So here I am, sister. Take your best shot."

Far from triumphant, the only thing Holly felt was tired. Funny, she'd looked forward to this moment for so many years and now... it just didn't matter. "Let's save the volleys for later. I could use a bite to eat. Join me?" She held her breath, uncertain whether the peace offering would be accepted, or not.

Confusion marred Susan's brow before she pasted on an attitude of indifference and shrugged. "Sure, why not? I don't have anything better to do."

With that ringing endorsement hanging like a gray fog, Holly swung around to head for the kitchen, only to become dizzy. She grabbed for the wall and closed her eyes, willing the weakness away.

"What's the matter with you?" Susan asked, her tone impatient even as an arm wrapped around Holly's waist to brace her up. "This is the second faint in twenty-four hours. Are you... *pregnant?*"

Holly gasped out a startled laugh and met her sister's concerned gaze. "No, I'm not pregnant. I don't even have a boyfriend."

Susan snorted. "What happened to Mr. Saxophone then?" Her eyes grew wide and she covered her mouth.

Holly straightened and stared at her in shock. "How do you know about Brian? Were you in New York?" And when Susan vigorously shook her head, "Did you have me followed?" She couldn't believe her family had done such a thing. Why?

Susan stepped back, allowing her arm to drop away only after assuring herself Holly could stand. "It wasn't like that. Levi has business in New York. He offered to check up on you, make sure you were doing okay. That's all, I swear."

Holly couldn't believe what she was hearing. Anger and indignation along with a healthy dose of *"what the hell?"* vied with a bruised heart. It was bad enough her family had never visited, but to send Levi to *spy* on her—unforgivable.

"I think you should go now," she said with quiet pride and lifted her chin, unwilling to let her sister know how deep the barbs had embedded themselves under her skin.

Susan stiffened as though she was the one under attack. "I should have known better. You're just as close-minded as ever." She stomped an icepick of a heel into their parents' hardwood floor. "How long are you going to maintain this holier-than-thou attitude, because I have to tell you, it's getting old."

Something inside Holly snapped. She reached out and gave her baby sister a shove. A thrill of satisfaction snaked up her spine when Susan screeched as her shoulders smacked the wall. "I'm not doing this right now. If you know what's good for you, you'll leave before things get uglier." Though how that could be possible, was anyone's guess.

She swept passed Susan in a righteous haze, the adrenaline from the encounter allowing her to march down the hall with barely a sway.

"You don't get it, do you?"

Susan's low pain-filled voice stopped her in her tracks. Holly swung around and found her braced against the wall, face pale and shoulders rounded. "Get what?" she asked, unwanted empathy forcing her to stay. Listen.

Susan stared a hole in the floor, beautiful blond hair lank around her face. "Did you know Mom never wanted kids?" She glanced up and away, her gaze moving to the crooked painting on the wall. "It's true. After you were born, she tried to make sure it never happened again, but oops, here I am." Her laugh came out as though forced through a shredder. "I tried, really I did, but I could never live up to you, the ingénue."

Holly froze, shocked to the core. Could this be true?

Random memories assailed her. Times when it should have been her in trouble, but Susan had been blamed. It hadn't been on purpose, she was no Miss Innocent, yet it sounded as though her sister hated her. Had wanted her to pay.

Steven.

"You slept with my boyfriend to get back at me?" The guilt that smudged Susan's eyes gave Holly her answer. She shook her head, stunned. "I don't know you at all, do I? Sisters are *supposed* to be there for one another. Someone you count on, no matter what. I remember holding you when you were a baby, and do you know what I felt?" Her fists clenched over her shattered heart. "Pride, Susan." She ignored her sister's flinch, intent on inflicting the same pain she'd received. "Pride that the beautiful little girl in my arms was my *sister*. I vowed then and there to always— always—take care of you and never let anyone hurt you. Ironic, isn't it?" She swiped the angry tears away. "The one person in the world I trusted, is the one to betray me."

Susan held up an entreating hand. "Holls, please."

Holly flinched at the childhood moniker, given to her when Susan was a toddler and couldn't get her name out right. Another carefully laid arrow? And that was the worst of it; how could she ever trust any of them again. They'd all told lies.

She gazed at Susan with new eyes. The young girl

she'd known, the one she'd loved, was nothing more than a figment of her imagination. And how sad was that?

SUSAN HAD WANTED to take out her frustrations on her sister, but she never meant to reveal her torrid affair. It was Steven's fault really; he'd made both Tremaine girls fall in love with him. At least, that was the justification she'd fed to herself for the last eight years.

None of it excused betraying Holly, though.

The way she stared at Susan with eyes that stripped the skin off her lies, laying them bare, flayed already bruised emotions raw. She grasped the doorknob digging into her back. She didn't need this; the kids had Christmas concerts this afternoon, Steven wanted her to pick up his suits from the dry cleaners, she still had groceries to buy and dinner to cook—

"Are you feeding me lunch, or what?" She was a masochist, that was the only explanation she had for staying instead of making good on her escape.

Holly's eyes widened, but she gave as good as she got. "Do you think it's safe?"

"I'll take my chances," Susan said, relaxing perhaps for the first time in months. The familiarity of their snarky, yet affectionate interactions brought back simpler, happy times. She'd looked up to her older, smarter sister and followed her everywhere. Where their parents were kind, if standoffish, Holly always had time for her pesky sibling.

Then Steven came along, and everything changed.

She released her death grip on the door and set the oversized satchel she'd assured Steven she had to have on the console table next to a cobalt blue glass bowl filled with porcelain fruit, before slowly following Holly. The closer she came to the kitchen, the more her limbs dragged. *Maybe this is a mistake.* She could come back later, when her parents were home to act as buffers. *Get a grip.* It was lunch not the Spanish Inquisition.

"Cheddar, Swiss, or mozzarella?" Holly mumbled, her head in the refrigerator.

"Hmm?" Susan said, bemused. Her mind was overloaded. The last few days reminded her of the fairground ride she'd talked Holly into trying when they were kids. They'd entered a capsule and buckled onto a narrow bench seat as the carnival worker closed the door with a screech that rattled nerves. At first, the gears moaned and groaned, the capsule shuddering as it picked up speed. Holly clenched the safety bar, her face pale but resolute while Susan remembered laughing—filled with so much joy and excitement she could barely contain it in her narrow chest. Then, without warning, the ride flipped them upside down, shaking like it was about to fall apart. Raw terror eclipsed the thrill. Susan was so frightened that when she screamed, little more than a whimper passed her lips. Somehow, Holly managed to reach over and grab her hand. She'd squeezed the blood from her fingers, but Susan didn't care; she held on to the only stable thing in a suddenly crazy, topsy-turvy world—her sister.

"Why didn't you ever tell Mother about the fair ride?"

Holly froze, then turned to face her, hands laden with eggs, cheese, an over-ripe tomato and green onions. She hip-checked the fridge door, letting it slide closed while juggling the items onto the kitchen island. Next, she rattled through a couple of cupboards until she found the right size mixing bowl and returned to the counter with a wicked-looking paring knife in hand. Chop. Chop. The green onions were diced, the tomato sliced, and the eggs added to the bowl before she answered. "You made me pinky-swear, remember?" She glanced up, then returned to beating the heck out of the egg mixture. "Besides, I could have said no."

But she hadn't.

The guilt that was never far from the surface rose, choking Susan. Her heart fluttered like a mad thing, beating itself against the wall of her chest in a futile bid for escape.

Escape.

She'd thought of running away so many times. Once, she'd even packed her bags, but it wouldn't be fair to Steven or the children. They loved their father, and he them. The issue was with her—and it all stemmed back to Holly.

"You must hate me," she said next, determined to get it out in the open. Cut the wound and let it bleed out. She feared it was the only way to heal her soul. Holly's vigorous mixing ground to a halt, and Susan wished for about the thousandth time that she could learn to control her inner voice.

"You're my sister, I could never hate you." Holly set the bowl down like it was a bomb about to explode. "Where is all this anger really coming from?" Then, in a hushed voice, "Are you and Steven having marital problems?"

Susan swung away from the sympathy in her sister's eyes. Her turn to open the fridge and stare at the surprisingly meagre contents. Couldn't her mother find the time to buy groceries, for Pete's sake? She grabbed the block of cheddar off the shelf and closed the door. "Did you see the grater while you were slamming cupboards?"

"I wasn't *slamming* them." Holly opened a cupboard and pointed above her head. "They never make kitchens for short people," she muttered.

Susan snickered, well aware Holly hated her short stature. "Dad told you to eat your beans." She laughed and reached for the utensil, only to still at Holly's expression. "What? Do I have lipstick on my teeth?" She rubbed at the enamel with her tongue.

"I haven't heard that laugh in so long." Holly blinked, and a curtain fell over her expression. "I want Swiss with my omelet."

The non-sequitur left Susan at a loss for words. The anger and the fear that had driven her to confront Holly had been replaced by nostalgia and a deep need to reconnect with her roots. There had to be a way to make up for what she'd done.

Even if it meant losing her husband.

CHAPTER
SEVEN

L evi forced himself to wait a couple of days before calling Holly. Much as he wanted to spend his time on the island with her, he realized she was here to reconnect with her family. It had taken tremendous courage to face the past the way she had; he only hoped her olive branch was accepted.

But, today, he planned to take her out of the city. A little away time to see how she was coping without the eyes and ears of her family watching their every move would be good for both of them. He dialed her number and waited, his gaze roaming the tastefully decorated hotel suite he'd rented for his visit.

"Hello?" she asked, hesitantly.

He had to clear his throat before answering, the visceral reaction of her voice in his ear catching him off-guard. "Holly? It's me, Levi. I was thinking you might need a break. Want to do something crazy together?"

She choked on a laugh. "Um, is it legal?"

He grinned at his reflection in the sliding glass window. "It's a surprise; you'll have to trust me." The words barely left his lips and he was wishing them back. What a *stupid* thing to say, given her experience with his brother. "Never mind," he said. "Dumb idea."

"Shouldn't that be my decision?" She sighed. "I can be ready in an hour, will that work?"

Unable to remain still, he rose and strode to the glass, staring down at the ships in the harbor. "I'm looking forward to it."

"Me too," she admitted. "See you soon."

"And, Holly... plan to do some walking." Levi's pulse skittered. Now, if only he could control his tongue and not say the wrong thing, they might actually get through the afternoon without an argument.

He hoped.

His phone rang in his hand and he answered without looking, expecting it to be Holly. "Chickening out already?" He smiled.

"Isn't that your forte, brother?"

Levi's good mood evaporated. "I'm busy, Steven. What do you need?" He set the phone on speaker and sat on the end of the king-sized bed to change his loafers to a pair of new hiking boots.

"Busy, doing wha...? Wait a minute, are you *seeing*

Holly?" His incredulous tone carried clearly across the line.

Levi frowned. Sometimes, it was annoying how well his brother could read his mind. "It's not a date, we're going for a hike. Is that a problem for you?" Steven had no right to be jealous; he'd made his choice a long time ago.

"Holly is... delicate. Do you think that's a good idea?"

"I *think* that you should concentrate on your own wife and leave her sister to me." Restless, Levi rose and paced the room, his toes crunched within the confinement of the stiff footwear.

Steven cursed under his breath, but it reverberated in Levi's ear. "I don't need marital advice from my bachelor-for-life brother. There's nothing wrong with Susan's and my relationship, so stay out of it."

"Take your own advice, buddy." He exaggerated the rattle of his keychain. "Gotta go. Talk to you later." He hung up with Steven's protestations ringing in his head. After his call, Levi was tempted to power down his cell phone for the rest of the day but resisted the impulse. Truthfully, Holly's fainting spells did worry him. Maybe a hike in the woods was a bad idea. He'd feel her out on the idea and see how she felt; they could decide from there. All he knew for sure was he wanted to be with her—the rest didn't matter.

As he left the hotel, the sun poked out from behind a band of fluffy cumulus clouds heating the December air. The valet drew up in his rental convertible and, after tossing the man a decent tip, Levi hopped behind the wheel. Already the tension began to fade away. He lowered the top, turned up the heat to counteract the breeze, and pulled out of the parking area, determined to make this a day to remember.

HOLLY BRUSHED out her hair and used a white scarf knotted under the heavy length to sweep it away from her face. A light blush to tint still-pale cheeks, a dab of lipstick and she was ready for her great adventure.

Her stomach fluttered at the thought of spending time with Levi. Alone.

She'd carefully blocked out their *mistake in judgement*, as she preferred to think of it, but the memories were making themselves known now. The day her sister walked up the aisle and said '*I do*' to the man Holly always thought would be *her* husband, had turned out to be harder than she could have imagined. Instead of cutting her losses and disappearing into the night, she'd sat through the entire affair—literally, as it turned out—without a clue to how it all would end.

Sleeping with the best man; how cliché.

Worse, in her drunken stupor she'd attempted to pretend Levi was his brother. Until he forced her to say his name in the throes of passion. She should have ended it there, but she didn't, and now that night was embedded in her brain.

And yet, here she was, butterflies and all, waiting by the front door like a teenager on her first date.

"Why in the world are you hovering like that, and what are you wearing?" her mother asked.

Startled, Holly whirled from peeking out the side-light window and stumbled over her backpack laying on the floor. "Mom, don't sneak up on people that way; you almost gave me a heart attack."

Claire raised her brow. "I don't consider walking in *my* home, sneaking. If you didn't have all of your attention on whoever you're waiting for, you would have heard me, I'm sure." She frowned at the door. "Where are you going?"

Holly debated the wisdom of telling the truth, then lifted her chin. "Levi invited me out for the afternoon. He should be here any minute now." *Hopefully.*

Claire fidgeted with the glass bowl on the hall table. "Do you think that's a good idea?" She glanced up, her gaze worried. "It could cause... complications."

For you or for me, Mom? Aloud she simply said, "It's just a drive. We aren't running away to get married."

"Holly, that wasn't necessary." Claire shoved the bowl and the porcelain balls inside clanged together.

"Do what you want, then. You always do." She turned and marched away, her back poker straight.

Holly stared at the misplaced bowl and blinked back tears. Why did her mother blame her for Susan's mistakes?

EIGHT

S usan parked her luxury SUV in the parkade and hurried down the busy street to the Drunken Lantern Pub and Grill. She blinked against the dimness of the bar and searched for her lunch date.

"Susie Q, over here," Nancy called, jumping up and down in her seat, waving like a lunatic.

Susan grimaced and slid between filled tables, feeling as though everyone was looking. She hated that silly high school name but had given up trying to get her best friend to graduate from using it.

"Sorry, I'm... late," she finished as she neared and realized Nancy wasn't alone. "Beverly, this is a surprise." She shot Nancy a glare and received a shrug in reply.

Beverly stood and gave Susan a perfunctory hug,

kissing the air next to her cheek. "It's been a while. You look tired, but then raising kids tends to wear one out, doesn't it?" she said with a snide look.

Before Susan could offer the witch a piece of her mind, Nancy swept her up into an enthusiastic hug and whispered, "Sorry, she invited herself," into her ear. The light jasmine perfume she wore was a stark contrast to the sickening sweetness of Beverly's scent.

Susan gritted her teeth and smiled as she took a seat, reaching behind her to hang her Gucci bag on the back of the chair. "It's been a crazy morning; I need a drink. How about you?" She waved a server over and ordered a glass of merlot. Nancy followed her lead, while Beverly chose a dry martini—no surprise there.

Customers at the tables around them laughed, talked and ate a variety of tempting-looking dishes while servers danced between a maze of chairs, trays laden with drinks or plates of steaming food balanced precariously over their heads. The Drunken Lantern had been built in the early nineteen-hundreds and had retained most of its charm. Milk glass chandeliers hung from a tray ceiling highlighted with thick crown molding. A polished bar fronted by leather-topped stools ran the length of one wall. Bottles of every size and description lined the glass shelves hanging on the wall and a group of fancy draft dispensers provided local craft beer. The floor was an intricate penny tile in shades of copper and green and a spiral staircase led up to a second floor that circled the outer edge of the building, allowing patrons to watch the action below.

Nancy was the first to break the awkward silence. "I have big news, are you ready? I'm getting married!" She bounced in her seat, face glowing with excitement. "Can you believe it?" She giggled.

"Yes, I do." Susan reached for her hand to get a look at the demure engagement ring. "Beautiful. Did Craig finally pop the question?"

She blushed. "He surprised me with a romantic dinner—got down on one knee and everything."

"He couldn't have splurged on a real ring?" Beverly said, gaze sardonic as she dipped an olive into her drink with a blood-red nail.

And you're here, why? "I think it's perfect," Susan announced, in response to Nancy's darkening expression. "Your fingers are so slim anything larger would be ostentatious." She eyed the rock on Beverly's hand. Black diamond, how appropriate.

"We're saving up for a house now Craig has his CPA certification. I'm so proud of him," Nancy said, but her tone was more subdued thanks to Miss Negativity.

The server returned to the table and they placed their orders; Island mussels for Susan, bacon cheddar burger for Nancy, and a goat cheese and cranberry salad—hold the dressing—for Beverly.

Susan toyed with her glass. She'd been a hot mess

on her wedding day, but then she hadn't had much support, either. She decided then and there to make Nancy's big day one to remember. "Do you have a date picked out yet?"

Nancy nodded, her cheeks flushing. "We, um, decided to wait until June. You know how tax season can be for accountants." She took a big swallow of her wine. "Besides, this way I'll have more time to plan, right?"

Beverly snorted. "It's not as though it'll be a country club soiree."

Nancy surprised Susan by reaching across the table to hug Beverly. "I'm so sorry, I wasn't thinking. This must be hard for you." She sat back just as their food arrived.

Susan waited until the plates were served before asking the question burning the end of her tongue. "What's so hard? What am I missing?" She hated being the last to know; it made her feel... unwanted.

Nancy looked uncomfortable. "It's not really my story to tell," she said, though she'd already blurted out the intriguing bits.

"It's nothing," Beverly snapped. "My jerk of a husband cheated on me and we're getting a divorce—no big deal." She downed her martini as though it were a straight shot of tequila and waved the server over for another round. "Now that's cause for a cele-bration, don't you agree?"

Susan's stomach plunged. This could be her if what she suspected was true. No wonder Beverly was bitter. "I'm—"

"Don't bother. He isn't worth it. I'm the lucky one." She pushed her chair back and rose, eyes bright. "Excuse me, I need to freshen up." Shoulders military straight, Beverly wound through the full restaurant, chin high.

"I should have kept my engagement quiet. I feel awful, now," Nancy said.

Susan squeezed her friend's hand, but her attention returned to the proud woman entering the ladies' room. "It's not your fault. Give her a minute, she'll be fine."

Her gaze roamed the pub filled with the downtown business crowd. Most seemed to be enjoying their lunch—unlike their table—except for a couple in the corner. Fiery red hair cascaded down a slim back. The rigid line of the woman's spine suggested she wasn't happy. Susan was about to turn away when the woman rose and a male voice she knew all too well carried across the room. "Tamara, wait."

Numb with shock, Susan stared as Steven hurried out of the restaurant after her, leaving his wife with a shattered heart.

CHAPTER
NINE

Holly held her flyaway hair to the side of her neck and enjoyed the crisp air blowing over her face. Levi had asked if she'd prefer to have the roof raised on the convertible, but the breeze was refreshing.

On the way out of the city, he'd stopped at a fruit market to pick up their lunch; fresh mango and pineapple, cheese and deli meats, water and sodas to wash it all down. Now, they were traveling west, darting around corners and drifting in and out of the shadows created by giant cedars and hemlock trees. The wind made it next to impossible to talk, which was just as well; she needed time to regroup after the confrontation with her mother.

The ocean played peek-a-boo with them, there one minute, gone the next; a deep azure that echoed her mood. Levi's earlier cheerful tone on the phone seemed a thing of the past, as well. He'd been considerate of her needs, but she could tell something was eating at him—what a pair they were.

The car clanked over a red steel bridge and Holly caught a glimpse of two trumpeter swans on the river below. Not long after, they passed through a small town obviously geared to the tourist trade with bed and breakfasts and businesses advertising whale watching tours and salmon fishing.

"It's been years since I was here." She smiled at Levi.

He glanced her way. "It's grown. We used to stay at one of the inns for holidays when we were kids. Steven hated it."

Holly could believe that. The Steven she'd known as a teenager loved sports and nightclubs in equal measure. He'd been fun and exciting compared to her more introverted personality. If she was honest with herself, she'd spent most of their relationship waiting for the other shoe to drop. She just hadn't expected her sister's betrayal.

A few miles further, Levi turned and drove down a winding country road that opened into a surprisingly large parking lot. The December sunshine had brought out other families and the lot was half full. Levi found a space and pulled in near the trailhead. He pushed the button and waited for the convertible top to close before shutting off the engine.

The sudden hush was disconcerting, and Holly cast about for something to say. "So, do you come here often?" *That's the best you can do? Lame, Tremaine.*

Levi chuckled. "You sound a tad nervous. Did you think I brought you here to have my dastardly way with you?" He rested a hand behind her headrest—his fingers a breath away from her neck.

All the hairs on her nape stood up, craving the promise of his touch. What was she doing? They were friends—or trying to be, anyway—she couldn't afford to repeat the same mistakes she'd made in the past.

She gave a nervous laugh and opened the passenger door. "Hardly. Come on, you promised me a hike, remember?"

He stared at her for a long moment, the humorous glint fading from his eyes, before he straightened and opened his own door and pocketed the car keys. "Yeah, sure. Prepare to be astounded by wild west coast beauty."

After years of big city living, the island felt like paradise, even with the tension at home. She waited at the back of the car while Levi grabbed the paper bags filled with their lunch items from the trunk.

He nodded toward the pack hanging from her shoulder. "Want me to take that? The path down to the water is steep."

Holly tightened her grip on the strap. "I'm good, thanks. Lead the way." It had taken perseverance, but she was slowly rebuilding her strength from the debilitating effects of chronic Lyme disease. At first, the simple exercise regime her specialist had recommended tired her out so much she'd quit doing them, which had the adverse effect of worsening her fatigue. *'Deconditioning'* they'd called it; she had a better name —frustration.

Levi kept a steady pace, glancing back frequently to check on her. She appreciated his concern, but at the same time it annoyed her. Would he babysit any of his other dates this way? Not that they were on a date, of course. Just two friends getting together on a sunny Saturday afternoon—yep, that's all. If only she could persuade her libido to quit drooling over his broad back and tight... jeans.

Then they cleared the top of the hill and she forgot to breathe. A panoramic vista of the Pacific Ocean lay before them in untamed glory. She realized now that the dull roar they'd been hearing before was the waves crashing against the shore; one upon the other in a never-ending drum roll of life. The sun glinted off the surface, turning the water diamond bright. She was glad she'd remembered her sunglasses and had brought sunscreen in her trusty bag.

"Beautiful, isn't it?" Levi said, grinning at her awed expression. "I think it's too early in the year, but we might get lucky and spot a gray whale. They migrate up north in the spring through the Juan de Fuca Strait. I've seen a few killer whales here, too."

She glanced at him, then quickly back to the scenery. Levi seemed as wild and untamed as the wilderness surrounding them with his tanned good looks and wind-tossed hair. It stirred an ache inside of her that she didn't want to acknowledge. She couldn't be attracted to Steven's brother, she just couldn't.

Needing to outrace her emotions, she started down the steep hill that would take them to the water. "Last one to the beach has to serve lunch," she shouted over her shoulder.

LEVI GUIDED Holly down the rocky beach, a hand on her back for support. The wind was chilly this close to the water and he frowned when she shivered, second-guessing his decision to bring her here. "Hold up for a moment." He set the bags down and pulled off his hoodie. "Put this on, it'll help."

She backed up a step, raising her hands to ward him off. "I'm fine, really."

Sure, she was. Her lips were turning blue. "Don't be so stubborn," he said, and dropped the shirt over her head.

"Hey," she cried, her voice muffled as she fought to find the opening.

He grinned when she finally got it on and cuddled into the warmth. "You look like a little kid in that thing. It's practically hanging to your knees." Not really. The sweater *was* too big, the sleeves hung past the ends of her fingers and was shapeless and bulky on her body. But the forest green color accentuated the striking golden-brown color of her hair and green-gold eyes. The hem cupped her thighs, highlighting trim legs in blue jeans with strategically placed holes in the knees and black boots with clunky heels.

"Thank you," she said. He didn't know if he was the cause for the pink tinge to her cheeks or the weather, but either way it looked good on her.

They'd stopped at a couple of tide pools to admire the intertidal biodiversity. Hermit crabs scuttled through the damp sand while sea anemones, urchins and starfish lounged in the cold water. Holly found shells she had to keep, and he spotted a piece of red sea glass that he gave her and was gifted with a radiant smile in return.

A giant sun-bleached stump of driftwood near the end of the stretch of beach drew his eye as a promising location for their picnic. "Hungry?" he asked.

"Starving," she admitted, straightening to stare out at the ocean. "It's beautiful. Thanks for bringing me here, Levi."

His chest warmed and he had to resist the urge to take her in his arms. Friends. That's all they could ever be, and he'd better remember that. "Sure. I don't know about you, but too much family time is hard on my health."

Holly turned her attention on him, tipping her head inquisitively. "I thought you and Steven were close?"

Uncomfortable, and kicking himself for saying anything, Levi shrugged. "We are, it's just that his priorities are different from mine and we don't always agree, that's all." He pointed toward the stump. "Shall we?"

She looked as though she wanted to say more, but instead nodded and started up the beach; a slim figure in an oversized sweatshirt.

He hesitated, then followed. It was hopeless to wish things were different between them, that she'd chosen him all those years ago, instead of his brother. Sometimes, he actively hated Steven. The guy could land in a pile of shit and still come up smelling like a rose.

"How's this?" Holly called, standing by a hollow in the stump.

She looked like the teenager he'd crushed on in high school, instead of the poised young woman he'd admired on a stage in New York. "Perfect," he answered, and he wasn't talking about their picnic site.

She helped him spread a blanket on the sand and unpack the bags. He offered her a soda, she accepted a water, and they both lounged back against the log and enjoyed the vista while chewing on ambrosia apples.

"Are you practicing your violin while you're here?" Levi asked and was surprised by the hurt darkening her eyes. He sat up and took her hand, lacing their fingers together. "What is it? I didn't mean to bring up painful thoughts."

She stared at their clasped hands. "No, it's fine. I'm... taking a break for a while." She lifted her head and met his gaze. "I heard you came to hear me play. Why didn't you let me know? We could have gone out for dinner or something."

Levi cursed under his breath. Steven, again. "It was a quick trip; I was there on business. Besides, your boyfriend might not have appreciated it."

"He wouldn't have had a say in it," she said tartly. "Well? What did you think?"

That you took my breath away. "You're good, Holly, real good," he said aloud. "They must be clamoring to have you back."

She laughed but there was no humor in the sound. "You'd think so, wouldn't you?" She broke their hold on the pretext of reaching for a slice of cheese. "And, what about you? Agent extraordinaire, I understand?"

His brows furrowed. She was prevaricating. "I do okay. Listen, Holly, if there's anything—"

"Look," she cried, jumping to her feet. "A whale. Oh, my gosh, did you see that?" She looked at him with sparkling eyes that clenched his heart.

He rose and wrapped an arm around her waist, watching her instead of the massive mammals breaching in front of them. "Stunning," he murmured.

CHAPTER
TEN

Susan couldn't remember how she ended up sitting in her car in the busy parkade. Vehicles pulled in, while others left with a squeal of tires on cement. There were families with colorful packages heading to their cars; businessmen and women in suits and dresses, briefcases in hand. Normal people going about everyday lives. How many of them were fools like her?

She'd invested all she was into her marriage. From the moment she'd seen Steven—back in high school—she'd wanted him. He'd been everything her young heart had dreamed of in the perfect man. Handsome, smart, fascinating.

A cheat.

If she was being honest, she'd spent the last ten years expecting something like this to happen. Nightmares peppered by her husband coming home with lipstick on his collar, discarded thongs in the backseat of his car, broken promises. In reality, Steven was a model father, a caring husband, a good provider. Where it should have eased her fears, instead they'd ballooned out of control. Without Jacob and Amy to keep her grounded, she didn't know what she would have done. They were her greatest joy.

How was she going to explain it to her children?

Damn him to hell.

She smacked the steering wheel. Again. And again. Each strike a counterpoint to the pain lancing through her chest. Big, ugly sobs erupted from her throat, a volcano of emotion over which she had no control.

By the time she settled down, shadows were creeping in through the open porticos. Susan read the clock through blurry eyes and gasped. She was late picking up the kids from school. Frantic, she dug through her bag, searching for her phone. Her fingers shook as she impatiently tapped through the passcode to access her contact list. The school came up under favorites and she dialed, praying someone was still in the office.

"Cedar Grove Elementary," a pleasant voice announced.

"Hel... hello, this is Susan Anderson. I... I'm running a little late. Is there any way my children, Jacob and Amy, could wait in the office until I get there?" She grabbed a tissue from the console and wiped her nose. "I'm so sorry. It won't happen again." In the background she could hear kids laughing and teachers talking. Embarrassment coursed through her body, though it was impossible for them to know her situation.

"Yes, of course," the admin answered. "I'll send someone to find them right away. What grades are they in?"

"Jacob is in grade three, French immersion. Amy just started kindergarten." Her breath hitched on the last word. Her daughter was little more than a baby— they both were—and now, because of that bastard, their innocence would be forever destroyed. She could have cheerfully killed Steven in that moment.

"Perfect. We generally release the older children first to avoid congestion on the playgrounds. They'll be here when you arrive. You won't be long, am I correct?"

In other words, they weren't childcare services. "No, I'm on the way now. Thank you." Susan hung up and lowered the visor. The woman staring back at her with red eyes and flushed cheeks would scare her kids. Time to clean up and put on the show of a lifetime. She would have to tell them sooner or later, but not until she could do it without bursting into tears.

Thankfully, traffic was light, and she made good time crossing the city. She even managed to come up with a temporary plan while making the drive. They were going to stay with her parents. The only fly in the ointment was her sister. But, surely, she planned to head back to the bright lights of New York and her all-important career soon. Until then, Susan would stay out of her way. She thought they'd had a breakthrough the other day at the house, but then Holly had shut her down and the moment was lost. No more. She was tired of being the mediator in her family. Let Holly step up to the plate for a change.

She tapped the Bluetooth call button on her steering wheel and asked for a connection to her mother's phone.

"Hello?" her mom asked as though she couldn't read her name on the screen.

"Hi, Mom. It's me, Susan." She signaled and turned onto the street with the school. "I was just thinking—the kids haven't had a chance to spend time with you in a while, and with Holly there... well, we'd like to come and visit." *Smooth, Anderson. Real smooth.*

Her mother tsked. "You know you're welcome any time, dear. When were you planning? Dinner on Sunday?"

Susan parked in front of the school, relieved to see the swarm of students around the building—not too late, then. "Actually, we'll be there tonight. We're going to stay over for a few days."

"Oh. Well of course, you can. There's plenty of

room." Mom cleared her throat. "Are you and Steven...?"

Fighting? Falling apart at the seams? Separating?

Dying inside? "We're fine, Mother. It's just a visit. Don't make a big deal out of it," she snapped, then immediately regretted it. "The kids want to see their auntie, that's all."

A gusty sigh later, her mom replied, "Well, if you don't wish to talk about it, there's nothing I can do. The children are always welcome. See you at dinner, then." Click, the line went dead.

Why did she feel as though she was jumping from the frying pan into the fire? Her mother had a way of conveying disappointment that managed to make Susan feel guilty, even when it wasn't her fault. She'd hated it as a child, and she didn't need it now. Her stomach had already twisted into a rat's nest of anxiety, was it too much to get some maternal support?

All the more reason to protect her own children.

She took a last glance in the mirror, patted her hair into place, and strode toward the office, head high.

CHAPTER
ELEVEN

The trip back to her parents' house passed in a contented blur. Holly couldn't remember the last time she'd enjoyed herself so much. Levi was the perfect host, gracious and sociable though he had to be curious why she'd come home now, after so long. How could she explain the growing urge to exonerate the past and restore family ties? Her sudden illness had taught her life was short—too short to waste on useless emotions.

"What are you thinking?" Levi asked, lips lifting in that familiar quirk that managed to do odd things to her pulse.

"How surprised I am that we got through the day without a single argument," she taunted, with a grin of her own.

He reached out and grasped her hand resting on

the seat between them. "I'm glad you agreed to come out with me," he said, his thumb caressing her palm.

She shifted until he released his hold, heat rising to her cheeks. "I am, too. I have to admit I didn't know what to expect."

He eyed her quizzically. "Did you think I planned to have my nefarious way with you?"

She laughed, but her girl bits quivered at the thought. "Don't be silly, I'm hardly your type." Levi pulled into her parents' driveway and parked. Holly fidgeted under his steady regard. "What?" She rubbed at an imaginary speck on her cheek. "Do I have dirt on my face?"

She stilled as he reached out and brushed a stray lock of hair behind her ear. The caress of his knuckles grazing her skin sent involuntary shivers chasing each other up her spine. His eyes darkened, the humor replaced by something she feared putting a name to. He couldn't be attracted to her; could he?

"Levi..."

"Shh," he murmured, leaning until their mouths were a breath apart. "You have the most delectable lips. I've been wanting to kiss them all day." He turned his hand to cup her jaw. "What do you say, Holly Anderson? Will you let me? I wonder."

He didn't wait for a reply. His mouth eased over hers and sent common sense flying out the window. He didn't rush, instead taking time to taste her as though she mattered to him. It was slow and sensuous, and she never wanted it to end. She moaned, helpless to hide the yearning he'd brought barreling to life. She touched her tongue to his, then withdrew, made vulnerable by the sensations coursing through her body.

"Levi," she said again, though she wasn't sure what she was saying anymore.

He moved his hand to her nape and tugged, drawing her into a seductive web she was helpless to escape. Didn't want to, even if she could.

"I've imagined this moment for so many years," he rasped, shocking her to the core.

How could that be? They barely knew one another. His kisses were like a drug, making it hard to think. There was something she should clarify, but...

A horn blared behind them. Holly jumped like a scalded cat, while Levi slowly, ever so slowly, eased back to his side of the vehicle. He started the engine and lowered the steamy windows, letting fresh air flow in along with awareness. They were making out on a public street like two teenagers in the throes of passion. What was she thinking? She hadn't been, that was the problem. An affair with Levi would never work. There was far too much water under the bridge between their families and her own drunken mistake ten years ago. In all reality, she was surprised he wanted anything to do with her.

"Umm, that was unexpected," she said, for lack of brilliant repartee. Her brain cells were still playing catch up with her hormones.

"But not unwelcome, if your response was anything to go by," he said quietly, watching her try to erase his touch from her body with fresh lipstick and a hairbrush. "I think we need to give this thing between us a shot, don't you?"

Flustered, she placed a hand on the door handle. "I'd better go. Thank you for the lovely time, Levi. I had fun."

He stared at her for a long moment, his expression holding a touch of... melancholy? Then he seemed to shrug it off, resorting to sarcasm instead. "Glad I could be of service, princess. Keep me in mind the next time you need an afternoon break, I might be available." He shifted the car into reverse and waited for her to get out.

Incensed, she turned back to refute his rude statement. "This *thing* is nothing more than the culmination of a pleasant day at the beach between two consenting adults." Her life was already as complicated as she could handle, adding Steven's brother to the mix was just asking for trouble. She needed her sister more than she needed a relationship—or so she told herself.

Without waiting for his reply, she climbed out,

closed the car door, and should have walked away, but tormented herself watching him leave instead.

It was for the best.

They lived on opposite sides of the continent and had careers to focus on—she hoped she did, anyway. They loved the same man. Levi, his brother. Holly, the guy she thought she'd marry.

It would never work.

HOLLY OPENED HER PARENTS' door to the unfamiliar sound of children playing. Little Amy squealed and ran down the hall to throw herself against Holly's legs, wrapping around her knees like a python. "Aunty, Aunty, we're sleeping with you."

Jacob followed more slowly, a shy smile on his handsome young face. "Not with her, silly. We're staying in our own room—with Mom."

Holly's heart quaked at the mention of her sister. She answered Jacob's smile with one of her own, but her attention was snagged by Susan leaning against the doorjamb to their father's office. She looked... tense. Her face seemed pale, her eyes dark and shadowed.

Steven.

She dropped her gaze, taking in the sweet innocence of her niece's upturned face. Her stomach roiled.

If anything had happened... "I think Grandma made cookies today. Why don't you go see if she'll give you one before dinner? Mommy and I will join you soon."

Amy's eyes lit up and she released her death grip to turn and run back the way she had come. "Hurry, Jacob. Let's go."

Jacob wasn't as quick to be bribed. He stared at Holly for a considering moment before turning to his mother. "Can we, Momma?"

Susan straightened and nodded. "Just one though, okay? Tell your sister."

He hesitated, then trailed Amy into the kitchen, leaving Holly in an all too familiar standoff with her sister.

"Out for a walk? You look flushed." Susan massaged her temple and closed her eyes.

Concerned, Holly took a few steps forward, then stopped when Susan's eyes snapped open. "Is something wrong? Is it Steven? Is he... *hurt*?" Her throat constricted. *Please, not that.*

Susan's laugh bordered on hysterical. She threw her head back and stared at the ceiling. "Your concern is touching, sister dear." Abruptly, she turned and headed for the den. "I need a drink."

Holly wished she'd ended things better with Levi. If he were here... but he wasn't, and she prayed he wasn't about to receive a fateful call. She could shake her sister, not that it would do any good. Susan was like a mule at times. She'd have to wait her out.

She tucked away her disapproval of the double shot of vodka her sister poured herself—slugging it back like it was water—but when she went to pour another, Holly stepped in, placing her hand over the cool glass. "Alcohol is not the answer, talk to me."

Susan's brows furrowed, her eyes red-rimmed. "Why do you care? It's no more than I deserve, right? The adulteress becomes the scorned wife—how cliché." She grabbed another glass and dumped the liquor in. "You can say it, I'm sure as hell thinking it. What goes around, comes around; that's what you forecast, didn't you? And you were so right." She sobbed into her glass. "So right."

Holly stared at her sister's agony and was filled with a conflicting jumble of emotions. Relief that Steven was fine—a jerk, but fine—satisfaction because it wasn't just her, as she'd feared all these years, and empathy. She'd lived through his betrayal herself, and knew how painful it felt, though Susan wouldn't want to hear that now.

All she could do was be there for her.

She set the half empty glass aside, wrapped Susan in her arms, and held on while her world crumbled around her. Maybe she didn't have the right words to say, but she hoped Susan could feel the love she craved to offer.

CHAPTER

TWELVE

D inner that night was a somber affair. Holly's parents were grim bookends at the table while Susan vacillated between misery and barely hidden outrage. The only bright spot at the table were the children. Amy swung her legs back and forth under her chair while she cheerfully told her grandparents all about her kindergarten class and how mean old Emily ended up with gum stuck in her hair. But it was Jacob who held Holly's attention. He listened to everything around him without drawing notice to himself. When his mom dropped her fork, he eased out of his chair to pick it up, offering her a clean one from the sidebar. And when Amy spilled a few drops of juice, he was there to clean it up, his eye on the disapproval radiating from his grandmother. The phrase, *still waters run deep*, came to mind as she watched him care for his family. He was a good boy, one who didn't deserve the responsibilities he would have to face in the coming days and months ahead. There were many things Holly could credit her sister with, but inner strength wasn't one of them.

She hadn't thought she was strong either, but she was learning differently.

"What are your plans now?" her mother asked, directing Holly's attention to the conversation.

Susan shrugged, her customary scowl making a return visit. "I told you, I'm not sure. It's not like I leave my hu…" She noticed Jacob's watchful eyes and substituted her words. "… *home* very often. I thought we'd spend a day or two with you and then maybe take a trip somewhere. How does that sound, Jakey? A vacation somewhere warm?"

Jacob picked at his food, moving each pea from one side of his plate to the other. "What about school? And Aunty Holly just got here, can't we go later?"

Holly reached over and squeezed his hand. "Maybe I'll have to go with you. What do you say to that?" The words tumbled out without thought but gained conviction by the time she was done. It would give her sister some much-needed support and the opportunity to know the children better. It wasn't like she had to hurry back to the orchestra—they'd said to take her time, make sure she was well before she returned. She would miss Levi, though.

"Jacob is right. It's hardly time to go on a trip, what with Christmas around the corner. Families belong *together* during the holidays," her mother said meaningfully.

"Maybe you should have shared that with Holly." Susan turned the attack her way. "*How many* have you missed?"

Holly flinched. It was obvious her sister was reacting like a wounded animal, but it hurt, nonetheless. "You're right," she said quietly "I should have made more of an effort, I don't deny that. But I'm trying now, if you'll give me a chance."

"And we're glad you're here, pumpkin, aren't we, *kids?*" Her father's pointed glance reminded them big ears were listening.

"Where's Daddy?" Amy asked, glancing around as though only just now noticing he wasn't there.

Holly took one glance at Susan's glowering face and leaned over to give her niece a spontaneous hug, inhaling the strawberry freshness of her hair. "He's working, honey. Did I mention how big you've grown? You're going to be taller than me soon." She smiled and kissed the soft, downy cheek.

Amy giggled. "*Aaa... unty*, that's silly."

Holly sat back and took a sip of her tea, disaster

averted. "I don't know about that. Do you realize I'm older than your mother, and yet I'm the short one?"

"Yeah, but you play music and Mommy doesn't," Jacob said, peering up through eyelashes any woman would love to possess.

Susan snorted. "That's because I was busy raising kids." She took a long drink of wine, eyes flashing with temper.

"Why does everything need to be a competition between you two?" Their mother scowled, glass of wine in hand.

"Maybe because you encouraged it," her husband chided.

Jacob's shoulders hunched. He stopped shuffling peas and squashed them instead. Holly frowned. Her sister was hurting, but if she wasn't careful, she'd end up just like their mother and lose her connection to her sister's children.

"Your mother used to be quite the dancer, Jacob." Holly smiled, remembering the times she'd played her violin and Susan had performed for their imaginary audiences, mostly made up of the girls' dolls and stuffed animals. Now and then, they'd had the opportunity to actually show off their talents at school concerts and the thrill would stay with them for days after. Holly missed the innocence of childhood.

"That was a long time ago," Susan confirmed,

pushing her half-finished plate away. "I haven't had a reason to dance in years."

"How about now, Mommy?" Amy hopped down from her chair to lean against her mother's side. "Aunty could play her violin and we could dance with you. It'll be fun." She broke away to twirl around the room, her skirt belling around knobby knees.

"Whoa there, Missy Mouse," Grandpa said, reaching out to slow her down. "No gallivanting around the dinner table. When you're done with your meal—including the peas—maybe we can talk your mother and aunt into putting on a little performance in the den, but not before. Deal?"

"Deal," both kids chorused.

Holly sucked in a deep breath and slowly released it. She hadn't played her instrument much since virtually receiving her walking papers. Nerves fluttered in her belly, reminding her of past pre-performance buzzes; of losing herself in the chords, the emotional wail the strings called forth, then building to a crescendo that reached in and tugged the souls of all who listened. The excitement of holding a concert hall full of people enthralled.

Yes, she loved music. For years after her breakup with Steven, it was her escape. But she'd give it all up if it meant having her sister in her life again.

SUSAN COULDN'T BELIEVE she'd been talked into *dancing* on the very night she left her husband—who hadn't even called to see where they were, not that she should be surprised. He was probably with that... that *woman*. She could barely think it without feeling her blood pressure skyrocket. The wail of the violin, as Holly tuned it before their so-called performance, seemed to echo the pain radiating in her heart. Sooner or later, she would have to face Steven with her accusations, but not yet. Not until she could do it without bursting into tears.

The moment Holly had opened the leather case and lifted the maple instrument from its red velvet nest, her expression had taken on a dreamy quality. It became an extension of her body, one lost without the other. Susan had always envied her sister's gift. Music was Holly's escape. Especially after...

"Mom, are you ready?" Jacob asked from his perch on the stool in front of his aunt. He'd been practically glued to her side all night.

Susan couldn't even use lack of space as an excuse; her father had grumped and grunted, but with a twinkle in his eye as he enlisted the children's help moving furniture back far enough to create an impromptu dance floor.

Amy clapped her hands and laughed, bouncing on her grandmother's lap. If Susan hadn't seen it with her own eyes, she'd never have believed it; her prim and proper mother playing tickle monster with her granddaughter. Her father watched them as well, tenderness stealing over his burly features. Her family.

Holly met Susan's gaze as her body began to sway, the melody changing from heartrending and mournful, to jaunty and upbeat. Lindsey Stirling. *She remembered.*

Almost with a mind of their own, Susan's feet took up the beat, tap, tap, tapping around the floor, arms raised as she pirouetted and whirled as though she could escape the boundaries of earth. And maybe she did—temporarily. One song flowed into another, and soon Amy and Jacob joined her, miniature *Tiggers* bouncing around the room. The only low point of the evening was when her father rose and held out his hand for her mother to dance and she shook her head in refusal.

Well, that and the phone call from Steven.

The vibration against her hip—she'd set the phone to mute after picking up the kids—was a death knell to the night's enjoyment. She was so tired of the roller coaster she'd been riding the past few years—she was over it.

"What do you want, Steven?" she asked, stepping out the back door for privacy. The faint sound of the violin and the laughter of her children was a warm counterpoint to the icy chill overtaking her heart.

"Where are you? I've been home for hours and was starting to get worried—and hungry." He chuckled.

Sure, you have. She wanted to chuckle herself but was afraid it might sound maniacal. "You'll have to make your own dinner. We're not coming home." Home. Her throat cramped with the stress of holding herself together.

He must have heard the tension in her voice, his next words were quieter, more intimate. "What's going on, baby? This isn't like you."

No. It was much more *like* her to roll over and play dead whenever he worked late or went on a business trip without his family because *face it, they'd just be bored.* She couldn't do it anymore. She just couldn't.

"It's over, Steven. I'm leaving you." She leaned her head against the door and stared up at the blue velvet sky. Serene when turmoil filled her chest.

He sighed, the hard-done-by male. "Is this about Holly? Look, I told you years ago, I *chose* you. You're being ridiculous."

She straightened, incensed. *Ridiculous?* Stupid, maybe. It had taken far too long for her to wake up to the truth, but she was an idiot no longer.

"Goodbye, Steven. You'll be hearing from my lawyer." She hung up on his sputtering and swiped angrily at the tears flowing down her cheeks. Funny, the satisfaction she should be feeling felt a lot more like desolation.

THIRTEEN

After he dropped Holly off, Levi was far too restless to go back to a barren hotel room. Instead, he drove aimlessly around the south end of the island, wishing she was there to take in the stunning vistas with him. The scenic Dallas Road curved from Fisherman's Wharf through Beacon Hill Park, Clover Point and Ross Bay Cemetery —a Victorian era burial ground. And all of it affording him jaw-dropping views of the Pacific Ocean. Victoria retained much of its old-world charm, whereas Vancouver had become an urban mecca for development. Not that he minded; his high-rise condo overlooking the city and mountains beyond gave him pleasure, and the nightlife was varied and entertaining. He never lacked for companionship, had even been in a couple of long-term relationships, but the restless gnawing in his gut never eased.

Until today.

Holly Tremaine was the complete opposite of the women he dated; introverted instead of outgoing, a little brown mouse to the sleek cats of the recording business. But he couldn't stop thinking about her. In truth, she fascinated him more now than when they were teens and she'd dated his brother. There was a depth, a melancholy, that drew him. Her smile had felt like a precious gift, as though she hadn't had reason to laugh in a very long time. It made him thirsty for more. He ached to banish the darkness from her eyes, but first he needed to know what put it there in the first place.

He parallel-parked along the sea wall and got out to stretch his legs. This close to the water, the wind whipped icy pellets that stung his face, reminding him Christmas was around the corner. A hot air snow globe bounced on someone's lawn across the street, the merry-go-round inside twisting and turning like a carnival ride gone mad. Nearby, a giant Santa figure in shiny black boots rocked forward and back, hands clasped over a belt buckle any rodeo bronc rider would pay to own. Out on the ocean, a couple of kite surfers were catching some serious air, rising twenty or thirty feet over the water before plunging down, their boards racing the waves until they could rise again. A crowd had gathered to watch the action. Levi grinned at a couple of boys mimicking the athletes, their arms spread wide as they sprinted over the grassy infield. He could remember himself and Steven doing much the same as kids. Good thing they'd outgrown their daredevil ways by the time they were old enough to flout their parents' rules—this sport looked like a bone-breaker.

He rubbed his hands together and brought them to his mouth to blow warm air into the hollow he made between his thumbs. Next time he'd remember to pack gloves. Next time—he was making plans to return, and Holly probably didn't care one way or the other. He was acting like a besotted fool for a woman he barely knew, it was... exhilarating.

His phone jangled in his pocket and his heart leaped, then dropped like lead when he read the caller's name—Steven. Briefly, he toyed with letting it go to voicemail, but sighed and answered, "What's up?"

"Where have you been all day, man? My life's imploding, I need you, bro."

The very real desperation in his brother's voice drew Levi up short. Steven always was a drama queen, but this sounded serious. "What's going on?" he asked, already striding back to his car. "Are you at the office? I can be there in half an hour."

"She left me, Levi. She's gone." There was a crash and then nothing.

"Steven," Levi yelled, heedless of passing pedestrians jumping out of his way. "Steven, answer me." But the phone remained ominously silent. "Shit," he swore and ran the last few feet to the convertible. Horns blared as he pulled into traffic, barely glancing over his shoulder. He crawled up on vehicles' bumpers —something he detested in other drivers—and raced through yellow lights, his brother's agony fueling his urgency. Steven loved those kids; this would destroy him.

He wasted precious moments driving over to the office, only to find it closed for the day. Back in the car, he had plenty of time to think while creeping along with the rush hour traffic. Whoever came up with that name, anyway? Rushing was an oxymoron for the crawl they were doing. He tried to call Steven back, but the phone just rang busy, and he contemplated ringing Holly to see if she had heard but discarded the notion. Better to get the facts straight before trying to solve the problem. He and Susan had never been close, but he couldn't see her running off without good reason, and knowing his brother...

Finally, he pulled into Langford and made the trek up Bear Mountain toward Steven's home. He didn't know what to say, especially if this was Steven's fault, but it was his duty to be there and act supportive. He just hoped it came down to a misunderstanding.

He ignored the doorbell in favor of banging his fist

against the heavy oak door. "Steven, it's me. Let me in." When that didn't work, he made his way around back, past the pool, and entered through the unlocked sliders. The silence hit him first. No laughing, chattering monkeys climbing his legs while his sister-in-law smirked from the sidelines. No aroma of the fresh-baked cookies she liked to make or silly cartoons playing on the oversized television Steven insisted on for sports.

But he did smell alcohol and it grew stronger the closer he drew to his brother's bedroom. The door stood agape and opened with a nudge. At first glance, the room appeared empty, but a groan from the far side of the bed quickened his step. Steven half lay, half sat propped against the mattress, an almost drained bottle of whiskey between his legs.

Sighing, Levi sank onto the floor beside him and gently pried the bottle away. "What are you doing to yourself, bro?"

Steven cracked open blurry eyes, hair falling over his forehead like a little boy's. "I tried so hard and she still left me, can you believe it? Clothes, kids, everything. Don't matter. Nothing matters anymore." He went for the alcohol, but Levi held it out of reach.

"You don't mean that. Let's get you cleaned up, then we'll talk, and you can tell me what the hell is going on. You don't just give up on a marriage, buddy. Not if you love each other. You do, right?"

Steven looked at him, his gaze riddled with pain. "You tell me," he said.

LEVI HAD a pot of coffee going and was in the middle of scrambling some eggs together with diced ham, tomato, onion, and peppers for a Denver omelet when Steven stepped into the kitchen. At least the shower seemed to have sobered him up some; he didn't have that death-warmed-over complexion going anymore.

"Hungry?" he asked, turning away to dump the mixture into a preheated pan.

"I could eat," Steven said, heading straight for the coffeepot. "Sorry about... you know." He shrugged. "Kind of caught me off-guard, I'm sure we'll figure it out." He kept his back to Levi and stared out the sliders toward the hills in the distance. "Maybe she just needs some time away, she's been crazy busy lately with the kids and all."

Levi nodded, though he figured there was more to it than that. Susan had never struck him as the flighty type; if anything, she micro-managed her family into neat little slots. One glance around this house told him she was an organization freak. There wasn't a cushion out of place; tough to do with two little kids running around.

"Maybe," he said, flipping the omelet. "When was

the last time you guys did something together—without the munchkins?"

Steven's laugh was hollow. "You're kidding, right?" He plunked his cup onto the kitchen island and pulled up a stool, ignoring the liquid he'd dribbled. "Between her schedule and mine, we're lucky if we even shared the bed at the same time."

Well, that could be part of the problem. Levi was no therapist, but even he knew a couple needed intimacy or the relationship would suffer. He dampened a dishrag by the sink and mopped up the mess before pouring himself a cup of coffee. "I think you need to talk to her," he reiterated his statement from the bedroom. "You can't give up."

Steven slammed his hands on the counter, then groaned as his expression morphed from outrage to agony. He held his head and rocked on the stool. "Remind me never to drink like that again; it's a young man's game."

Levi snorted. Since when was thirty-three considered old? He pulled a glass out of the cupboard, added a shot of the whiskey he'd confiscated earlier, three spoons of runny honey he'd found in the pantry, and two equal portions of milk and cream. He stirred the lot together and set it in front of his brother. "Here, try this."

Steven looked at it dubiously. "What is it?"

"Hair of the dog. It'll either fix ya or kill ya." He chuckled.

"Ever the comedian," Steven groused, but he picked the glass up and downed the drink in one swallow, shuddering afterward. "Ugh, that stuff will burn my guts out."

Says the guy who was drinking straight whiskey an hour ago. "You'll live," Levi said. "Ready to eat?"

"Not if it tastes like that," Steven retorted. He grasped Levi's arm as he was about to turn away. "Thanks, man. I'm glad you're here."

Levi stared at the features so like his own and his throat closed up. They might not always get along, but they were family. In the end, that's all that mattered. "Get the plates, would you? I'm not doing everything for you."

Holly kept playing though her mind wasn't on the music. One moment, they'd all been enjoying themselves, and the next Susan had taken a call and disappeared out the back door. Amy and Jacob were fizzing out after all the excitement, their eyes over-bright and cheeks flushed. Holly decided to play the aunty card and get them ready for bed.

"Who wants to hear a story before bedtime?" She smiled when they lifted their hands and cried, "Me, me."

"Okay. Let's get you washed up and into pyjamas and I'll see what I can come up with—sound good?"

Off they went, racing each other down the hall to the room they were sharing with their mother. The den suddenly seemed oppressive without them and she jumped when her father stood. "I have some work to do in the office. Leave this until morning, I'll get it then." He squeezed her shoulder and lumbered out without a glance at Claire.

She twisted her hands in her lap, then rose, preparing to leave as well. "Goodnight, then. This was... nice."

After that startling compliment Holly wasn't anxious to rock the boat, but she needed to know, "Mother, are you and dad separating?"

She froze, then bent over to fix a couple of cushions knocked out of place by the children. "This isn't the way I wanted to tell you, but... yes." She straightened and lifted her chin. "Just so you know, it wasn't my idea. Your father needs *space*, he tells me, whatever that means. Now, I'd rather not speak of it over the holidays, if you don't mind." She smiled, though it broke Holly's heart. "Go now, the children are waiting."

Holly rose and before she could second-guess herself, impulsively hugged her mother's unyielding frame. Just as she was about to let go of the broom-stick-like hold, her shoulders slouched and curled around Holly's slighter frame, soaking up the comfort she freely offered. Tears threatened, but Holly valiantly held them back. If her mom could remain strong, so could she. Besides, Dad would be lost without her mother. He just needed a reminder.

"I'll talk to him, make him realize he's making a mistake," she said, holding on for dear life.

Her mother wrenched free and stared her down, breasts heaving. "You will do no such thing. This is between me and him. I do *not* need my children to fight my battles."

Well, all right then. "Fine, have it your way. Maybe if you were caring instead of judgmental, he wouldn't be in such a hurry to leave." She turned away, refusing to feel guilty for speaking the truth. "I'll go read to the kids now. At least they want my help." She glanced back as she reached the door and her heart clenched. She'd never seen her mom look so defeated.

THE HOUSE WAS quiet when Susan re-entered. Shivering slightly, she confiscated one of her mother's embroidered sweaters from a chair in the den. Too restless for bed, she began reorganizing the furniture that had been left stranded on the fringes of the room and paused when she came to her sister's violin, lying open in its case on the foot stool. Funny that it should remind her of herself, with its frayed fretwork and air of abandonment. She slammed the lid shut and turned away, her stomach hollow. She wasn't alone; she had her children, friends, family. Just because her husband was going through a crisis of idiocy didn't mean her value as a woman was gone. Steven could take his little bimbo and... and, stick her.

She crumpled onto a chair and bent over, burying her face on her knees as sobs ripped her heart to shreds.

Sometime later, she became aware of a faint murmur creeping down the hall. She sniffled, dried her eyes on the cardigan's sleeve, and rose, the urge to hold her children compelling. The door to her bedroom was propped open and she was about to enter with the intention of chastising them for talking instead of sleeping when she heard Holly's voice.

"More than anything the princess dreamed of seeing her family for Christmas, but she feared they wouldn't feel the same way."

"Why, Aunty?" Amy asked. "Doesn't her mommy love her anymore?"

"Don't be silly," Jacob inserted. "There's lots of reasons why families aren't together for the holidays."

My wise little boy. Susan propped against the wall, just out of sight, curious to hear what her sister would say next.

"It's not silly at all," Holly chastised. "The princess had been gone for a long time. She was scared her family would be too angry to welcome her home. So you know what she did next?"

"Tell us, tell us," both kids chorused.

Holly laughed. "Well," she said. "The princess

thought long and hard, and then she decided to follow her heart. She flew home the very next day, and do you know what happened then?"

"Aaaaaunty!"

"Okay, okay. Tough crowd." The room erupted in giggles and Susan peeked around the corner, catching Holly's eye as she tickled the kids' bellies from their perch in the middle of the king-sized bed. Jacob noticed her preoccupation first and turned toward the doorway, a gap-toothed smile lighting his face.

"Mom," he cried, and hopped from the bed, raced across the room, and into her arms. He'd had a bath. His hair was still damp and curling at the ends. His superhero pyjamas were soft and fuzzy, and his little boy scent enveloped her with love and tenderness. No matter what happened, she would always be grateful to Steven for giving the gift of her beautiful children.

"Hi," Holly said, her expression sobering as she climbed from the bed. "I was keeping the kids company until you came back. I'll get out of your way now."

"But, Aunty, what about the princess?" Amy asked, a pout on her lips.

Susan nodded. "Yes, we all want to know. What happened to the princess?" Though she had a good idea.

"Well," Holly said, tapping Amy's bottom lip with her finger. "She apologized to her family for what she'd done and asked them to forgive her. And then she made a *big* batch of gingerbread cookies and they all lived happily ever after."

Susan's chest tightened. She'd forgotten their family tradition of baking before Christmas. Their mother used to fill the kitchen with cookies, then she and Holly were set loose with the sprinkles and icing. When Santa came to their house, he'd never gone hungry.

She cleared her throat. "Okay, you two, time for bed. Kiss your aunt goodnight."

Amy stood on the mattress and wrapped skinny arms around Holly's neck, squeezing her in one of her surprisingly strong bear hugs. "Night, Aunty. I like your princess story."

Holly closed her eyes and leaned into the hold. "Thank you, kiddo. I do, too." She tucked Amy under the covers, then faced Susan. "Your kids are wonderful."

Susan tightened her grip on her son, for once in agreement with her sister. "You should have seen them as babies. I spent hours dressing them up."

"*Mom*," Jacob groaned, and squirmed to get down.

They shared a grin as he crawled in next to his sister, then Holly met her at the door. "I wish I'd been here; they truly are precious. I hope you'll let me make it up to them." She met Susan's gaze, her eyes dark pools of regret, and then she was gone.

CHAPTER

FIFTEEN

L evi finished his dinner and took the dish to the sink, giving it a quick rinse before stowing the plate into the empty dishwasher. Steven didn't know how lucky he had it; a clean house to come home to, a wife who loved him, children—all things Levi wanted, but hadn't found the right woman to share them with.

He turned and leaned against the counter. Steven still carried that morose, poor-me look, but at least he was sobering up. Maybe now, he could get some answers.

"Ready to tell me how you threw away the best thing that ever happened to you?" Might as well lead off with a punch.

Steven reared back, nearly toppling off the stool before he righted himself. He glared at Levi. "Of course, you'd assume it's *my* fault. What happened to innocent until proven guilty?"

Ah, the lawyer at work. "Show me the evidence and I'll believe you," he said, and gestured around the room. "At the moment, all I see is an empty house and a drunken idiot who feels sorry for himself."

"I don't..." Steven stopped and rubbed a frustrated hand behind his neck. "Okay, I do. But only because I have no idea why she left. We were fine this morning; she was getting the kids ready for school and I was running late so I skipped the breakfast she'd made me —shit, do you think that's why?"

Levi's brow rose and he crossed his arms. "Do I think your wife left you because you didn't eat your breakfast? What are you, *two*?"

Steven shot him an incredulous look. "And Mom said you were the smart one? Maybe it's because I've been so busy with the new office? With all the stress I haven't been as focused on my family as I could have been, but they should understand. I'm doing all of this for them."

Levi wasn't so certain. Steven had a compulsive personality. Whatever he took on, he had to triumph, whether it was sports, school, or winning the girl. Holly came to mind. It drove his brother nuts to be second-best at anything. But after close to a decade of living together, Susan should know that about him. He had a feeling this was different—serious.

"Well, you won't know what's going on until you clean yourself up and go talk to her. Where is she, anyway?"

Steven shrugged, his brows furrowing over the alcohol-induced headache he was no doubt sporting. "A hotel? Maybe her parents place? Hell, if I know. This is bullshit. I don't expect to work myself to the bone, only to have my wife walk out on me. We have a big dinner coming up this weekend, what am I supposed to do now?"

There was that whiny kid again. Levi turned away to pour another coffee and give himself time to get past his brother's egotistical attitude. It was probably worry, more than selfishness, but that kind of arrogant attitude wouldn't win him any points with Susan. If he could even get her to listen.

Levi shut off the machine, drained the pot, and replaced it on the hotplate before facing Steven again. The guy was a wreck. His hair was mussed, tie cock-eyed and shirt half-unbuttoned, as though he'd planned a shower until receiving the life-changing phone call. Unbidden, empathy welled. Levi wasn't sure what he could do, but somehow, he had to try. If there was one thing he was certain of, it was how much his brother loved his children. Would it be enough to give his marriage a second shot?

"Look, maybe I could talk to her, test the waters, so to speak. Are you sure you have no idea of why she'd leave you?" Levi took the discarded plate and repeated the rinse, stow away process while Steven rose and paced his living room.

"If I knew I could do something about it—this hit me out of the blue." He stopped and stared at a portrait of Susan and the kids hanging over the mantle. "I want my family back."

Levi walked over and wrapped an arm around his brother's shoulder. "I know you do, buddy." Whether he could get want he wanted remained to be seen.

HOLLY COULDN'T SLEEP. Her room seemed to echo the silence—so different from her sister's room. Wonder what they'd think if she knocked on their door and asked to join them? She grinned at the thought, imagining the children's delight and Susan's glower. She'd enjoyed herself today; first with Levi, and then the first family home evening in far too long. Even her mother and father had tabled their differences for the night—mellowed by their grandchildren's presence.

And Susan danced.

Holly closed her eyes, picturing the dreamy movements, her sister swept away by the music. She'd always been a talented dancer, but experience had added another element, almost ethereal. She remembered when they were kids and Susan had planned to open her own studio while Holly fantasized of the symphony.

Only one of them had reached their goal.

Maybe that was part of Susan's dissatisfaction. There was little doubt she loved her children and her husband, but it was equally obvious she loved to dance. Holly's eyes snapped open. That was it. She'd done well during her time with the orchestra and tucked most of her money away for a rainy day—she could help her sister achieve her dream. She just had to figure out a way to get her to accept the gift, especially since they weren't exactly on talking terms.

Her phone pinged with an incoming text;

Awake? Thinking of you.

Holly smiled. *Are you flirting with me, Levi Anderson? How did you know it was me? Osmosis?*

She giggled, then covered her mouth and glanced at the door like a teenager hiding from her parents' wrath. *My phone shows me who's calling, silly. Why are you still up? I would have thought all that fresh air would knock the city boy out.*

Appreciate your faith in my libido, truly.

Holly sputtered. *You're incorrigible.*

I've been told. I had fun today.

Butterflies took wing in her stomach. She turned onto her side and cuddled into the fluttery sensation. *Me too. You're a nice guy.*

She held her breath and watched the three dots blink on her screen.

Ouch, the kiss of death. I wouldn't have taken you for a cruel person, Holly Berry.

Ooh, the flutters were on the move. She shifted under the covers, her skin sensitized. No one had ever given her a nickname before. She was much too plain and reserved.

Cat got your tongue?

The smile widened. *I was trying to come up with an adequate response, but silence works. Better to leave them guessing, right?*

Is that part of the dating handbook?

Holly's pulse jumped. Dating, is that what they were doing? *Quit teasing, Levi.*

Nothing.

Nothing.

Her heart clenched. She'd gone too far. He'd had enough. Then the three dots appeared.

Come out with me tomorrow. I want to see you, again.

The air whooshed out of her lungs. Could they do this? Forget their past and try a relationship? She didn't know, but that wasn't going to deter her.

Okay.

SIXTEEN

L evi took his seat in a corner of the eclectic diner Holly had chosen and waited for her to make an appearance. He'd offered to pick her up, but she'd insisted on making her own way—Miss Stubborn.

The restaurant was packed with an assortment of age groups. It seemed the overly loud music and almost frenetic energy of the waitstaff didn't bother the seniors gathered around a large table tittering like a bunch of teenagers. Prints of various rock and roll icons covered the walls in a hodge-podge of shapes and sizes that nevertheless all came together in an overall welcoming design. Judging by the plates a server had just delivered to a nearby table, the meals were monstrous, and made his mouth water.

Holly appeared in a cranberry peacoat with matching felt hat and everything else faded to the background. He rose to catch her attention and answered her smile with one of his own.

"Hi," she said, her voice a bit breathless. "Sorry I'm late."

He held out her chair and inhaled the jasmine scent of her hair as she slid into her seat. He resumed his place and stared, fascinated, as she removed the hat and coat to reveal wavy chestnut hair and a distracting forest green tunic. Belatedly, he realized she was watching him expectantly. "I'm glad you're here," he said, and meant every word.

She stopped fiddling with her clothes and looked at him through her lashes. "I was surprised to hear from you last night after the way we parted."

"Were you?" he asked. He reached across and waited until she took his hand, his pulse jumping at the contact. "It would take more than a little argument to keep me away. Besides, I owe you an apology."

She took her hand back and placed it in her lap. "No, it was me. I didn't handle your... proposal well. But in my defence, you surprised me."

The server, a perky blonde with a gold stud in her nose and a tattoo of birds taking flight on her neck, dropped off a couple of menus and said she'd be right back. Holly watched her flit between tables to a pile of plates steaming under a heat lamp, and Levi watched Holly. Her reticence was a cloak she hid behind like a safety net. She didn't need to protect herself from him, but that was something she had to learn with time. He'd cut off his own hand before he ever deliberately hurt her. He wasn't his brother.

"What were you wearing last night when I texted?" he asked, hoping for one of her precious smiles. "It's hard to fantasize without a fully realized image in my head—though my imagination was having a field day." He grinned.

Her eyes widened and she glanced from side to side before leaning over the table. "Shh, people are going to get the wrong impression."

Oh no, they were definitely going to get it right— at least from his perspective—but he could see he was making her uncomfortable, so he let it go for a safer subject. "Did you have a nice dinner with your parents? They must be happy to have you home."

She relaxed and picked up the menu that read like a book. "It was nice, thank you. Susan and the children were there, as well. They're adorable. It makes me doubly sad I stayed away all these years."

So that's where Susan had gone. His instinct was to call Steven and let him know, but another side said his brother deserved to stew for a couple of days. It wouldn't hurt him to gain a little appreciation for what he had. Levi could test the waters though—see if a reconciliation was even possible.

"Did Susan say anything to you about her and Steven?" He grimaced at her surprised look. "Sorry, I suck at diplomacy."

Holly set the menu down and stared at him. "Why? What's going on?"

Shit, he'd let the cat out of the bag.

He sighed his relief when the server appeared. "Ready to order?" she asked, her smile friendly.

Holly ordered a light breakfast and he went for the full meal deal, then waited while she topped up their mugs with coffee before disappearing to place the order. The restaurant had filled up while they'd been talking, and the noise was a welcome buffer to what he had to say.

"Well?" Holly repeated, her eyes dark.

What if he told her and she went running to Steven? After all, they had history. He hated his doubts, but they were there anyway, like poison arrows hitting their target. Still, if he couldn't trust her, what kind of relationship could they have? Still, Amy and Jacob needed their parents. He had to focus on priorities and let the cards fall where they may.

"Your sister left my brother. I need help getting them back together—you in?"

~

Holly stared at Levi, shocked. And hurt. No wonder Susan looked so stressed. That explained why she'd spent the night at their parents' house when her own home wasn't far away. Here, Holly had thought she was trying to make amends, spend some sisterly time together—she should have known better. And what about Steven? He must be devastated—unless...

"What happened?" she asked, twisting her fingers into pretzels. *Please, let this be salvageable. Please.*

Levi frowned after a couple of young men who accidentally bumped her on their way out and apologized. "Idiots," he growled.

"I'm fine," she said, mopping up the spilled coffee. "Never mind them, how's your brother holding up?"

His scowl deepened. "He was recovering from a bender when I left him."

"Poor Steven," she murmured, her heart squeezing with sympathy for the kids. Marital separations were hard on everyone, especially the children involved. She had friends who'd split up and the kids became pawns in ugly court settlements. She'd hate to see that happen with Amy and Jacob.

"I knew it," Levi said, leaning back in his chair and crossing his arms. "You never got over him, did you?"

Startled out of her reverie, Holly refocused on his grim visage. "What are you talking about? This has nothing to do with me. In case you've forgotten, I left town years ago so that the rumors would end and Susan could enjoy her marriage. Steven and I were done long before they spoke their vows. *You* should know that better than anyone." Dammit, she'd slept with the man, hadn't she?

He put his hands up. "Whoa. Methinks the lady doth protest too much."

She looked at him and sighed. "You're right. I guess it comes from defending myself so much back then. It was tough to play the *'it doesn't matter'* card in front of all your friends and family when it did. It mattered a lot." She tipped her head and studied him. "In fact, you're the only one who wouldn't let me wallow in self-pity. Why was that, Levi?" He was also the one to make her forget Steven on his wedding night—however briefly.

Levi shrugged and picked up his coffee. "Maybe I thought you could do better," he murmured. "Anyway, back to our current issue. Any chance you could talk your sister into a meeting with Steven? He swears he doesn't know why she left. I'm hoping this is all a big misunderstanding and we can be back to status quo by Christmas, for the children's sake."

Their server returned with piping hot dishes of food stacked mountain high. Holly looked at her plate, then Levi's, and burst out laughing. "If we get through all of this, we won't need anything more until Christmas."

Levi grinned and dug in. "I'm willing to take one for the team."

Holly opened a jam packet to spread onto her toast, but inside she wondered how they were going to bring their two stubborn siblings together before the holiday.

CHAPTER
SEVENTEEN

Susan woke late and in a strange bed. Startled, she sat up, taking note of the bland beige paint and heavy oak door—her parents' home. Yesterday's events flooded back in a torrential wave that brought tears to her eyes. She sniffled and looked around for a tissue, freezing when she noticed two blond heads burrowed under the covers. Strange for Amy and Jacob to still be sleeping, they were normally up at the crack of dawn. Steven often called them his little roosters. She reached out and gently touched cool brows, relieved they weren't coming down with something. They had enough on their plate this Christmas.

Leaving her kids to sleep, Susan rose, donned her bathrobe and quietly left the room in search of coffee.

The house was quiet. She assumed she was alone until her father spoke from behind her.

"Good morning, daughter. Thought you might sleep the day away."

She jumped, nerves on edge, then relaxed and turned to smile at her dad. "You used to tell us that all the time as children."

"I remember," he said, a twinkle in his eye. He looked around. "Where are the little ones?"

She tightened the belt on her robe. "Sleeping. I guess having a sleepover agrees with them."

He put a comforting arm around her shoulders. "Well, you know you're welcome here for as long as you want."

She kissed his bristly cheek. "Thanks, Dad. I just need some time to figure things out."

"Come on," he said, guiding her toward the kitchen. "Let's see if the old battleaxe left us any coffee. I have something I want to say, but I can't do it without some fortification."

Not only had her mother made them a fresh pot of coffee, she'd set out a continental breakfast as well. Plump raisin bran muffins competed for tray space with cranberry scones and thick slices of banana bread. Juicy red apples and pink grapefruit filled a fruit bowl along with thick clusters of red and green grapes.

Susan poured the coffee while her father set out dishes and napkins. "Quite the feast. If she keeps serving us like this, the kids will never want to go home."

"Believe me, this is all for you. I'm lucky to get a dry piece of toast when we don't have company."

Susan chuckled. "Poor daddy, it looks as though you're fading away." She patted his healthy belly. "I think Mother feeds you just fine."

"Hmph," he snorted, and reached for a slice of banana bread. "I won't deny she *did*, that is before she got it in her head things needed to change—whatever that's supposed to mean."

Susan idly wondered if there were classes men signed up for that taught hang dog techniques. Steven courted the very same expression when he didn't get his own way, and even Jacob had attempted it a time or two, though she was still able to bribe him out of his doldrums.

She joined her father at the table and sipped her coffee and nibbled on a muffin while he finished his breakfast. She was hesitant to bring up her parents' marital problems, but since he'd opened the door on the conversation— "I've, uhm, noticed you two haven't been getting along so well, recently. Have you tried counselling? Maybe if you talked it out..."

He slowly and methodically wiped his fingers on the napkin, then took a drink and stared into his cup as though it carried all the answers. She wished it were that easy.

"I didn't mean to interfere," she said, uncomfortable with the silence. "It was just a suggestion, ignore me."

"Do you remember when you were young, and we all used to sit around this table every Sunday for dinner?" He ran a gnarled hand over the equally tarnished wood surface. "Your mother wanted to buy a new, more fitting, table when we moved to this house, but I wouldn't let her." He pierced Susan with startling blue eyes. "Without our memories, what do we have, really? A fancy house, a nice car, those are all well and fine, but at the end of the day home is where the heart is and that means family." He took her hand and held it between his. "This thing between you and your sister has gone on for long enough. Make peace with her, daughter, before it's too late."

Too late? What did that mean? Was Holly ill? She'd asked the day her sister had almost fainted and received a non-answer in reply. To her lasting shame, she'd been too busy pulling the self-righteous act to delve any further. More than anything, Susan wished Steven was there to make things right. He'd always had a way of seeing through a problem and finding a solution. It's why he'd managed a successful career in family law. She missed him with every beat of her heart—maybe she was making a mistake.

"Is Holly all right, Dad? It's just... she hasn't been home in years, and last night was the first I've seen her play the violin since she came back. That's not the Holly I remember; you had to take it away in order to get her to sleep." She smiled at the memory.

He nodded. "I recall another little girl who liked to sneak a flashlight under the covers so she could read to all hours of the night; any idea who that might be?"

Susan smirked. "I got away with it, too."

"Only because you fell asleep not long after," he clarified.

She sat back, surprised. "How did you know? All this time, I thought I outsmarted you guys."

He chuckled and reached for a cluster of grapes. "Not with the way you snored. Now, about Holly." He chewed on a piece of fruit before continuing. "You didn't hear this from me, but she's taking a break from her music, I'm not sure why. That's another reason I want you to end this ridiculous feud between the two of you. She used to tell you everything. I think she needs a confidante."

Susan played with the crumbs on her plate. It wasn't that easy. The *feud*, as her father put it, was her fault. If she hadn't tricked Steven into being with her all those years ago, she wouldn't have betrayed her sister and lost the best friend she'd ever had.

EIGHTEEN

After a filling brunch, Holly left Levi and drove to a nearby beach. She'd spent many happy hours contemplating life while bird watching and listening to the tides roll in. It usually left her calm and meditative—today, not so much.

Levi confused her. Impossible to deny his charm. He was a handsome man, one she wanted to get to know better. Sooner or later they were going to need to have an honest conversation about *that night*. She shivered and wrapped her coat around her body. She'd drunk too much, she remembered. Watching her sister marry Steven... it was hard. She'd held it together through the interminable lead-up to the big day, had smiled through the ceremony, though her jaws ached from clenching her teeth, had even given a speech at dinner as maid of honor—ironic, that. But standing back while he'd taken his beautiful bride in his arms for the first dance killed her. She could have left then, should have, but instead she'd let pride get in her way and vowed to stay to the bitter end—with help from the open bar. She wasn't a masochist.

Then Levi showed up at her side and one thing led to another. They'd slept together that night and she'd run away the next day. So adult of her.

A group of cormorants sunned on a bleached length of driftwood, their long black wings glistening as they preened. Ducks floated on the currents, pintails, mallards, and goldeneyes sharing the nutrient rich waters of the lagoon with the larger geese, seagulls, and occasional swans while eagles soared overhead. She'd missed the island so much. New York was amazing but it couldn't compare to the pristine beauty of the Pacific Northwest.

She sat up and stared out of the windshield of her father's car. She was done running. She was going to do her level best to help her family and then she was going to find a place here, on the island, and get back to her musical roots. There, she had a plan.

Now to put it into action.

Holly started the borrowed car, carefully backed onto the narrow two-lane road, and set the navigation to take her to Steven's office. It was time for them to talk.

LEVI PULLED up to Steven's in-laws' house and shut off the convertible. He'd always liked this neighborhood with its blend of old and new. Some of the homes were giant Victorian monstrosities, and then there were ones like the Tremaines' with its understated elegance. The street was lined with giant oak, hawthorn and Japanese cherry trees creating a peaceful canopy and privacy for the yards.

After meeting with Holly this morning, he'd decided to take matters in his own hands and pay a visit to Susan. There was only one way to find out what was going on and that was by hearing both sides of the quarrel. He just hoped she was willing to see him.

He was about to ring the bell when the door opened and Claire stepped out. "Oh," she said, her eyes wide. "You startled me, Levi. What are you doing here?"

She was one of the few people who never mistook him for his brother. "Hi, Mrs. Tremaine. I'm here to see Susan, if she's available."

She gave him a penetrating look. "It's Claire, dear. I believe we've known each other long enough to skip formalities. Besides, you're practically family." Her eyes flickered and he could almost read her mind. *"For now, anyway."*

"Yes, ma'am," he said, taking note of her paleness. "Are you okay? You seem... "

"Agitated?" she supplied, tugging a pair of skintight leather gloves onto long, narrow fingers. "I suppose I am. It's not every day that a woman... well, never mind about me. Go on, coffee is in the kitchen. I believe Susan is there with her father. I have *no* idea where my other daughter disappeared to, but then that's nothing new."

Before he could answer, she slid past him and hurried down the walk, a woman on a mission. Levi stared after her until she disappeared from view. It bothered him that Holly and her mother were obviously at odds. One more ruined relationship he could trace back to his brother. Steven had a lot to answer for.

Claire had left the door open, so Levi stepped inside and removed his jacket before making his way toward the kitchen. He faltered at the entrance, noting Susan and her father having what seemed to be a serious discussion at the breakfast table. He should have called first, or better yet, waited for Holly to speak with her sister—he was actually surprised she wasn't here. He couldn't blame Susan if she kicked him out, anyway. He had no business stepping into the middle of anyone's marital issues.

He'd taken a careful step backward, intending to

leave, when she glanced up and froze, her expression filling with such naked hope it was painful to see.

"Steven?" she stammered, half-rising from her chair.

Cursing his stupidity, Levi smiled and walked further into the room, out of the shadowy hall. "Not quite. It's his thoughtless brother, dropping in without an invitation. Hello, Susan. George. Your wife let me in on her way out, I hope you don't mind?"

George waved him into a chair, either ignoring, or oblivious to, his daughter's shock. "How are you, my boy? I'd assumed you'd returned to Vancouver after our dinner the other night."

Levi accepted the seat, studying his sister-in-law out of the corner of his eye. Her fingers trembled around the coffee cup she'd grasped like a lifeline. She was still in her robe and her blond hair was mussed as though she'd just climbed out of bed. Vastly different from the put-together young woman he was used to seeing.

"I'm well, thank you, sir. I had some downtime coming and decided to stay on until after the holidays. It's been a while since I've spent much time with my family." He sent Susan a friendly look she attempted to return with a shaky smile.

"Young ones these days, they spend too much time worrying about the future to enjoy the present." George shook his head and grunted as he rose. "Well,

I'll let you two talk. It's time I get outside and stretch these legs of mine." He squeezed Levi's shoulder. "Don't get old, son, it's a pain."

Susan waited until her dad left the room before rising to pace, her steps short and body language stiff. "Sorry about my father, the winter wetness affects his joints." She stopped on the far side of the kitchen and swung around to face him. "Why are you here, Levi? Did Steven send you?" Again, with the hopeful lilt in her voice.

Levi wished he could agree but lying wasn't going to solve whatever was going on between them. "He doesn't know I'm here," he admitted, frowning when her shoulders slumped. "But that's only because he wants to talk to you himself." A fib, not the same as lying at all.

She shook her head, loose strands flying around like Medusa's snakes. "It doesn't matter. I have nothing to say to that... that philanderer."

Damn, he'd been afraid of something like this. He was going to kick his brother's ass when he saw him again. He rose and strode over to take her resisting figure into his arms. "I'm sorry, honey. I know this is hard on you and the kids." He cupped her shoulders and leaned back to meet her tear-wet gaze. "Are you sure? Could it be a misunderstanding?" He had to ask, though he hated to put her through more pain.

She broke away and swiped at her cheeks with

shaking fingers. "I don't think I've cried as much in my whole life as I have the last few days. I saw them together. Yesterday." She shrugged, misery in the movement. "I've had my suspicions; he's been distracted, receiving phone calls at all hours of the day, and night, and I accepted—" Her laugh was harsh, ripped from the depths of her soul. "—*accepted* his excuse of work. He must think I'm the most gullible person on earth."

Or I am. Levi had believed the story of a wronged husband Steven had pulled on him. He'd better have one hell of a good explanation or...

"Not what you expected?" Susan held her hands out. "Once a cheat always a cheat. After all, he's done it before."

Maybe, but something didn't fit. His brother loved his wife and kids. More than once over the years, Levi had envied them their closeness as a family. He couldn't see Steven throwing it all away on an affair. He hoped he was right.

CHAPTER
NINETEEN

Holly pulled into the side lot next to a beautiful old Victorian renovated into offices. She was surprised by the location of Steven's business. Retail space was bound to be expensive in the up and coming James Bay district.

She stood on the sidewalk and stared at the tasteful sign directing clients to enter for Accredited Family Law Mediator - Steven Anderson. Butterflies beat their wings against the walls of her stomach, as anxious as her feet were to run the other way.

She stiffened her spine and reached for the door handle, just as a young woman pulled it from the other side. "Oh, I'm so sorry," she cried, her voice tremulous.

Holly stepped back to let her exit, concerned with the woman's skittish behavior. "It's my fault, I wasn't watching where I was going." She held out a hand to stabilize the stranger, if needed. "Are you okay?"

The lady reached into her voluminous coat and came out with a tissue. She wiped her nose and took a deep, wavering breath. "I will be, thanks to Mr. Anderson. My husband is suing for full custody of our children, it's been horrible."

Empathy for the woman's plight squeezed Holly's tender heart, though it concerned her that this could be her sister if Steven decided to take the same recourse. She couldn't let that happen.

"So, is St... Mr. Anderson your lawyer, then?" Holly delved, curious to find out what the boy she'd loved was like as a man.

The woman nodded. "He's been helping me for the last month. The hearing is next week." She blinked away her tears. "He told me not to worry, but..." She gave a watery laugh. "I'm petrified."

Impulsively, Holly gave the lady a swift hug, hoping to instill strength for the coming ordeal. "It'll be okay," she whispered. "Have faith." She stepped back and gave a reassuring smile.

"Thank you," the stranger-who-wasn't-a-stranger anymore said. "I'd better go. Good luck." She hoisted her shoulder-bag under her arm and hurried off down the street—a lonely figure against the backdrop of colorful holiday decorations covering the storefronts.

Holly gazed up at the sign once more, somehow

reassured by the brief exchange. Taking a deep breath, she entered her brother-in-law's domain.

The entry was warm and welcoming, the floors a dark hardwood that matched the wainscoting, while the walls were painted a soft gray pearl. A woman looked up from her computer at the reception desk and smiled. "Hello. May I help you?"

Holly tamped down the urge to make a run for the door and stepped up to the counter. "Is Mr. Anderson in? I'd like a moment of his time, if I may?" She stood her ground under the woman's assessing gaze.

"Mr. Anderson has a busy schedule. Who might I say is calling?"

Holly glanced around the empty waiting room and raised an eyebrow. "His sister-in-law."

"Oh." The woman gasped. "Well, that's different then. Go ahead, dear. He's just working on case files. I'm sure he'll be thrilled to see you." She smiled.

Holly wasn't so sure about that, but she nodded and strode with what she hoped looked like confidence toward the door with Steven's name emblazoned in brass, her heart tripping over itself.

He stood when she entered; his face running a gamut of expressions from surprise to pleasure to wariness. Smart man.

"Holly, this is unexpected." He crossed from behind an ornate desk and came towards her, arms outstretched. "How are you?"

She closed her eyes and took in the familiar comfort of his touch. He seemed taller, his shoulders strong and broad, but none of that mattered, she'd know him anywhere. *Steven*. The good news—instead of having her heart take flight, there was only the pleasant glow of friends reuniting. Progress.

She patted his arms and backed away on the pretext of removing her coat. While he closed the door, she set it on a low leather sofa facing a brick fireplace and strolled to the large bay window facing the ocean across a busy street.

"Nice place," she said, turning with a smile she couldn't hold inside. Their history was a warm, slightly threadbare blanket between them, the threads still strong, though time and wear had created holes she hoped could be repaired.

He glanced around with a self-depreciating look. "Not bad for the class goofball, right?"

"No," Holly murmured. "Not bad at all." She cleared her throat and crossed her arms against his charm. "I'm here about Susan. Are you cheating on my sister, Steven?" She cringed. She'd never been one to beat around the bush, but this was a new low, even for her.

Predictably, he stared at her, shocked. "Where the hell did you get that ridiculous idea from?" His head reared back. "Susan?" Visibly shaken, he jerked around, then turned to nail her to the floor with laser-blue eyes. "And you believed her. Tried and convicted without a trial, how disappointing."

She couldn't blame him for his sarcasm, she'd hit him with her accusations out of the blue. But, a tiny voice whispered, he didn't deny it, either. "Look," she said, sitting in one of the guest chairs and then bouncing up again because of the disadvantage it gave her. "Susan is justifiably upset. She says she saw you with a woman at a restaurant the other day. Did she?"

He ignored her and walked over to a group of framed certificates on the wall behind his desk. "Do you know how long it took me to become an accredited lawyer?" He glanced at her over his shoulder. "Jacob was in kindergarten." He touched the glass, then sank into his chair with a tired sigh. "The woman is a client, Holly. You might even have seen her yourself. We just finished an appointment shortly before you arrived." He aimlessly twirled a pen on his desk. "I spend every waking moment trying to get this business off the ground—I don't have the time, or the inclination, to cheat. That's not me." He froze and lifted his gaze to hers. "Not anymore."

The thing was, she believed him. He didn't come across as a guy trying to cover up his indiscretions, more like a man doing the best that he could for his family. Now, she had to figure out a way to prove it to her sister.

"Okay," she said and picked up her coat, anxious to leave so she could think.

Steven rose and strode to her side to grasp her arm. "That's it? Okay?" He gave her a little shake. "You can't come here and accuse me of something like that, then simply leave. It doesn't work that way." He grabbed the coat and held it aloft. "You're not leaving until you tell me what you're going to say to my wife."

Stunned, and a little annoyed, she placed a hand on his chest for leverage and lunged for her jacket. "Don't be an idiot. Give me my coat."

Undeterred, he twisted his upper body to the side, so the jacket was out of reach. Unfortunately, it knocked Holly off-balance and she fell into his arms just as the door opened behind them.

"What, in the name of all that's holy, is going on here?" her mother roared.

CHAPTER
TWENTY

Holly pushed away from Steven, rattled. "Mother, what are you doing here?" She shot him a thanks-for-nothing glare when he handed over the coat.

Claire closed the door at her back and stared at them with eyes so icy they froze Holly's blood. Oh, no, no, no. This wasn't good.

"Mom—" she pleaded, unconsciously reaching out to the woman who'd cuddled her when she'd fallen off her bicycle and scraped her knee, but there was no break in the stern expression.

"It's not what you think," Steven inserted, clearly exasperated. "We were just... catching up."

Chicken. He was clearly intimidated by her mother. Holly gritted her teeth. "I came to Steven over a *personal* matter I'd hoped he could help me with, that's all."

"Well, that's *not* what it looked like when I walked in," her mother said, tugging off dark leather gloves, like finger by finger exclamation points. "You're lucky it was me who found you, *catching up*, and not your sister."

Lucky, yeah right. Holly held her stomach. Stress wasn't good for her condition. Her head was pounding, and she felt dizzy. To make matters worse, she'd misplaced the backpack she carried her medications in.

Fed up, she blurted the truth. "Susan thought Steven was fooling around on her, that's why she brought the children to you. And I had this idiotic idea of coming down here to try and get them back together before the holidays. End of story."

Claire looked up from removing her gloves. "I know my daughter, Holly. One of them, anyway. Obviously, she was upset and needed some time to think— why else would she look so... lost. I want to know if she's right." She smiled grimly at Steven. "Are you disrespecting this family and your wife by having an affair?"

No," Steven sputtered, his face turning an unflattering red. He scraped his hands through his hair and pulled, as though trying to evict the women from his mind. Holly could have told him good luck with that.

Once the Tremaines burrowed in, there was no escape.

He swung around and stomped over to a drink cabinet, hidden discreetly in an alcove. He popped the top off a crystal decanter and lifted it, offering them a drink. Holly shook her head, then wished she hadn't when the room spun like an out of control merry-go-round. When things settled, Steven had capped the bottle and was striding across the floor with a drink for her mother. Who never drank before four o'clock. The world was turning topsy-turvy.

It suddenly dawned on her to question her mother's appearance. "Why are *you* here? Don't tell me you need a lawyer." She laughed, but it died an aborted death at the look on her mom's face. "Mom?"

Claire took a sip of the alcohol, gave a slight shudder, then set the glass on a table by the door bearing a bouquet of hydrangeas and a holder filled with business cards. "Your father and I are considering a separation. Steven has been kindly guiding me through my options. It's as simple as that."

Simple? Her parents had been married thirty-five years, there was nothing *simple* about them getting a divorce. Holly frowned as the room wavered in and out of focus. This was all her fault. If she'd stayed on the other side of the continent, her family would still be together.

Her legs turned to rubber and she collapsed. Her

mother's shocked face rushing toward her was the last thing she saw before she fainted. Her fault.

SUSAN STEPPED out of the shower and stared into the steamy mirror. The woman looking back at her wasn't the one Steven had fallen in love with. This body wore the mantle of childbearing with wider hips, a scar from Amy's forced cesarean, a belly more round than flat, full breasts rather than perky—in a word, mature. She was mature. So why did she feel like curling into a fetal position and ignoring the world? If only it were that easy to escape life's bombs.

She sighed and finished dressing. Levi had agreed to stay on and watch the children while she got cleaned up, so she'd better get moving. Sometimes, she wished she'd fallen for the other Anderson brother. Levi was a good man. He always had time for her and the kids. He would make some woman a wonderful husband. She often wondered why he'd never married.

By the time she returned to the kitchen, Amy and Jacob had finished breakfast and were ensconced at the table with coloring books and crayons. They each had to show off their art, a unicorn for Amy, and a firetruck for Jacob, before she was able to refill her coffee and join Levi sitting on a stool at the island.

He glanced up, smiled, then held up a finger while finishing a text to someone on his phone. A minute later, he returned the gadget to his pocket and pushed the sugar bowl her way. "Sorry about that, I have a new talent on the hook and don't want him to squirm away while I'm gone."

He seemed so relaxed whenever he visited, it was easy to forget Levi ran a busy agency. He'd helped many new musicians make a name for themselves within the industry.

"Do you ever wonder if you're doing what you're meant to do?" she asked, clanking her spoon back and forth in the cup.

"How so?" he asked, his gaze on the twirling liquid.

Clink, Clank. Clink, clank.

"I just wonder if it's too late to make some changes. I've been a wife and mother for most of my adult life, I feel... invisible, I guess."

Levi reached over and covered her hand resting on the counter, halting the pendulum motion of the spoon. He waited until she lifted her eyes to his. "Being a mother is one of the hardest jobs out there. You're responsible for your children's health, welfare, and the values they'll carry through life. If that's not important I don't know what is."

He squeezed her fingers before letting her go. "That said, if there's anything I can do to help, just ask.

After all, you're my favorite sister-in-law." His lips quirked.

She smiled, the hard knot in her stomach loosening. "You're incorrigible. I'm your only sister-in-law." *At least for now.*

"See," he said, rising to refill their cups, "you win every time."

Amy hopped down from her seat and ran to her uncle, waving the coloring book like a banner. "I'm all done, Uncle Levi, can I put it on the fridge now?"

Ahh. Sneaky, Uncle Levi. He caved under her daughter's cheeky smile and ripped out the colored unicorn, moved a magnet holding a shopping list to the front of the refrigerator, and got Amy to help him place her picture right in the center. Susan hoped her mother didn't mind a few fingerprints on her shiny chrome appliance.

"What about you, Jacob, almost done?" Her heart tugged whenever she looked at her beautiful boy. He was a miniature image of his father with his serious expressions and fathomless blue eyes.

He glanced at his sister's work, then nodded. "Just about, Momma. I want to make it perfect." Another aspect he shared with his dad; he had to be the best.

Her father wandered back into the room. "Whoa-ho, what do we have here? I didn't know we had artists in the family." He rubbed Jacob's curly head, duly admired the bright red firetruck, then looked at Amy's unicorn with a rainbow horn on the fridge. "Just what we need, Amy-doll, a unicorn. Maybe it'll bring us some luck, what do you think?" He picked up his granddaughter and smooched her cheek before setting her back down.

Amy giggled. "Can I watch cartoons now, Mommy?"

Susan tried to monitor how much television her children watched but decided an exception could be made with the disruption to their normal schedules. "Okay but keep it down."

The sound of the television drew Jacob's attention and it wasn't long before he excused himself to join his sister. Her father picked at the leftovers from earlier, but Susan could tell he was upset. "What's wrong, Dad?"

He frowned. "Thought I'd run into your mother outside, but she was gone. Dang woman has a bee in her bonnet—not sure what she plans to do."

That sounded ominous.

"Don't worry, she probably just needs some space. I'm sure it's nothing." Says the daughter with an imploding marriage.

He snorted. "I told her *I* needed space. I thought that would shock her out of this silliness. Instead, it's made it worse." He pushed the plate away, ignoring the scraps that dumped over the side. "I don't know what to do."

Susan looked to Levi for advice, but he only shrugged, clearly uncomfortable. Her parents couldn't divorce, they were the anchors in their family. Without them, she feared they would all spiral apart.

"Dad—" The house phone rang, thankfully interrupting the moment. Her father waved her to answer, so she hurried over to the handset resting on the counter. "Hello?"

"Susan," Steven said, his voice sending goosebumps up her spine. "It's your sister. She passed out in my office. The ambulance is taking her and your mother to the hospital."

The words faded in and out. Holly and Steven. Hospital. Her mother.

"Susan, did you hear me?" Steven demanded. "She needs you to be there when she wakes up. Do you need a ride?"

She snapped out of her fog. "N... no. Levi can drive me. Will she..."

"I don't know, honey," he murmured. "You'd better hurry."

She clicked off the phone and turned to face Levi and her father to find they'd both risen and were now inches away. "Hol... Holly fainted," She stumbled over the words, her stomach clenching with fear. "They're taking her to the hospital. I knew something was wrong. I should have pursued it. She was with Steven."

And she wasn't going to consider what that might mean right now.

Levi's face was grim. "I'm just as guilty. She mentioned she hadn't been well the other day and I let it slide. Come on, I'll drive us there and then we can find out what's going on."

"What about the kids?" Susan cried, on the edge of panicking. "I can't leave them here alone."

Her father grasped her arm. "We're family, bring them."

CHAPTER
TWENTY-ONE

Holly woke with a dry throat and sore head. An antiseptic scent, the soft swish of feet in the hall, and the beep-beep of a nearby monitor informed her of the location before she opened her eyes. She was in the hospital. She lifted her hand to rub her forehead and frowned at the tube taped to her arm.

"You were dehydrated," her mother said. "They have you on a saline drip."

Holly rolled her head on the stiff pillow and met her mom's worried gaze. "How long was I out?"

"Too long," Steven said gruffly from the end of the bed. His knuckles were white where they gripped the foot board. "You scared your mother. What the heck happened?"

Holly closed her eyes and swallowed, the dizziness

gone, but she was still overwhelmingly tired. "The doctor didn't tell you?"

"She said we had to wait until you were awake." Her mother's tone stated what she thought of that. "Here, maybe this will help." She handed a blue plastic tumbler over, filled with slivers of ice.

Holly gratefully accepted the glass and sighed her pleasure at the instant relief the ice brought to her throat. "Thanks," she croaked. "I didn't mean to worry you."

"Well, then, how about explaining why the doctor seemed to feel we should know about your illness." Her mother sat back and folded her hands on her lap. "If you'd mentioned something was wrong, we might have been better prepared to help you."

"Claire, I'm sure Holly didn't want to worry you," Steven admonished. He straightened as the door whispered open over the polished tiles and Susan entered, ushering the kids in first, with his father-in-law and Levi following close behind.

"Daddy, Daddy," Amy sing-songed, skipping across to her father's open arms. He scooped her up for a hug, then smiled at his son.

"Jacob, have you been taking care of your mother and sister like we discussed?"

Jacob nodded solemnly. "Yes, sir."

Steven kept his grip on Amy and held out his hand, smiling as Jacob's much smaller one disappeared into his grasp. "Thank you, son. Now, how about giving your Aunt Holly a hug? She's not feeling too good."

Holly copied Steven's smile and forced her body to cooperate enough to lift her head from the pillow and snuggle into her nephew's teddy bear hug, inhaling his fresh, clean little boy scent.

"Okay, that's enough, kiddo. Give her room to breathe," Susan said, coming up to the side of the bed to frown down on them like an avenging angel.

"He's fine." Holly reluctantly loosened her grip. "I feel better now that my favorite kids are here."

"Why do you have a needle in your hand, Aunty?" Amy asked, her eyes wide. Steven let her down and she slid closer.

Holly turned her wrist so they could get a better look. "Truthfully? A bug bit me a while back and it makes me not feel so good now and then. This needle is helping by feeding medicine to my body. It doesn't hurt," she assured them.

Her mother rose and stared at her. "You have Lyme disease?"

Susan gasped. "Why didn't you tell me?"

Steven's frown deepened. "Susan, really. Try and have some sympathy for once."

She turned on her husband. "Don't you tell me how to feel."

His chin rose. "Someone has to."

"That's enough," Holly's father growled,

lumbering up to the end of the bed. "This is no place for petty squabbling. What is this *Lyme disease*?" he asked, squeezing her leg reassuringly.

"Oh, George, do you live under a rock?" Claire snapped. "It's caused by the bite of a tick. The symptoms can mimic the signs of flu: aching muscles, headaches, fever, chills, fatigue. Left untreated it can cause problems for years." She leaned over the bed and surprised Holly with a kiss on the forehead.

Levi had quietly made his way to the other side of her bed. He pushed the lever so that the head of the frame lifted, allowing her to relax against the pillows. She gave him a grateful glance. "Thank you."

"Glad to see you with color in your cheeks," he murmured. "That must be good stuff they're feeding you, there." He nodded toward the beeping monitor and half-empty bag of liquid dripping through the tube.

She nodded. "If I hadn't lost my backpack with the medications I need to take, this wouldn't have been necessary."

He lifted his arm and a dark blue backpack dangled from his fingers. "Do you mean this bag?"

Holly stared, confused. "How did you...?" Then the light went on. "The road trip. I left it in your car," she said. "Damn."

He grinned. "At least I found it before I returned the car to the rental place."

Her stomach dropped. She ignored the muttering from her family going on in the background to look at this man who'd come to mean so much to her. "Are you leaving?" Of course, he was. His life was in the big city pursuing a successful career. She was... a distraction, that's all.

He glanced at his brother, then shrugged. "Nothing really to keep me here, is there?" His dark eyes seemed to be saying something else entirely, but she put it down to the drugs they were feeding her. He couldn't be attracted to her, could he?

The door swished open again, and the doctor with an entourage of interns entered the room. "Full house, I see." Her smile was gentle, but firm. "I'm sorry, we need you all to step out now so we can treat the patient. There's a cafeteria on the main floor, if you care to wait." They stood aside as Holly accepted her family's manhandling while taking their leave. "And we would appreciate if you could keep it to two or three visitors at a time. Hospital policy."

Holly stared as everyone slowly traipsed out of the room. Her mother stopped and spoke quietly to the doctor before glancing back at her, and then she, too, was gone leaving Holly trapped in a cloud of blue and white coats.

TWENTY-TWO

Susan herded the children out of the hospital, her heart beating uncomfortably hard at the touch of Steven's hand on her back.

"We have to talk," he murmured in her ear, sending a cocktail of reluctance and anticipation to swirl around in her stomach. Was this it, then? Did he plan on telling her he'd found someone else? She'd get the kids every second holiday and spend the ones alone like a crazy old cat lady waiting for tidbits of her ex's new life.

She twisted free of his hand and caught up to her mother. "Will you take Amy and Jacob home with you? I'm going to catch a ride with Steven."

Claire searched her eyes. "Are you ready for this?"

No. The word welled up from the depths of Susan's

soul. Aloud, she said, "It'll be fine, Mom. I won't be long."

Claire turned and they both watched as Steven and Susan's father took Amy's hands and swung her back and forth between their bodies. She giggled and drew smiles from an elderly couple sitting on a bench near the entrance. An ambulance backed up to the side-walk, lights flashing, and two paramedics bailed out, ran around to the back doors and off-loaded a man strapped to a gurney. They lowered the wheels and hurried him into emergency, the IV bag, attached to the bed, waving like a flag above their heads.

"I realize you're old enough to make your own decisions, but I think you should listen to what he has to say. Really listen," her mother said. She gave a short, sharp nod and strode away to round up the children.

Jacob, in his solemn, solid way, walked over and tipped his head up until Susan crouched next to him.

"What is it, honey?" She brushed a curl off of his forehead and buttoned his coat against the chill.

He shrugged, his button nose, with its splattering of freckles, red. "I want to go with you," he muttered.

She tipped her head, surprised. "I thought you enjoyed spending time with your grandma and grandpa."

"I do." He shuffled his feet and kicked at a pebble before meeting her gaze. "But I don't want you and Dad to fight. If I'm there you won't, right?"

Susan's throat clenched and she had to blink back tears. "Jacob, you argue with your sister, now and then, but it doesn't mean you don't care about her. Adults are the same way. I love your father, never doubt that, okay?"

He stared deep into her eyes as though weighing her words, then wrapped his arms around her neck and squeezed tight. "Love you, Mom."

Her heart swelled. "Love you, too, Peanut. Now get going. You know how impatient your grandmother can be." She let him go with a watery smile. They may have taken a wrong turn, but she and Steven had raised smart, kind, beautiful children. Jacob had made her face a truth that she'd hid beneath her hurt—she loved her husband.

She rose and waited while he helped her parents load the children into Levi's car, and a determination to save her marriage grew in her breast. They could work through their differences, they had to. Steven was her soul mate.

He was silent on the ride back to their home, his jaw forbidding. Now that the time had come, she didn't know where to start, what to say to make this distance between them disappear.

He pulled into their driveway and shut the engine off, then sat staring out the front windshield. "You hurt me, Susan," he said, at last, turning accusing eyes her way. "I wrongly assumed we were a team, and then you pulled the rug out from under me with that phone call. What the hell was that about, anyway?"

On the defensive, she lashed back, her good intentions flying out the window. "What did you expect? Who is she, Steven? Did you think you could keep a girlfriend on the side, and I would be too stupid to figure it out?" Spittle flew from her mouth and for once, she didn't care. Decorum be damned.

He jerked back and his head smacked the side window. He stared at her as though it was her fault, his hand rubbing the injury. "What in the Sam hell are you talking about? There's no girlfriend. I can barely afford the family I have, why would I go looking for another one?"

Indescribably hurt, her heart in shreds, Susan fumbled with the door latch and stumbled into the house. If that's how he considered their relationship— as a measure of how much they cost him—there was nothing left to say.

She strode into their—his—bedroom and flung her suitcase on the unmade bed. It bounced and almost tipped on the floor onto her toes before she caught it. Angry and sobbing so hard she could barely see, Susan began packing, her life condensing into one square box of clothes.

Turning for another load, she hesitated on Steven's grim face as he stood watching from the doorway. She rubbed her nose and eyes with the back of her arm and stomped into the walk-in closet, frowning when he followed her into the small room.

He held his hands out as though to tame a wild beast, and she had to admit the analogy was apt. "Honey, you need to calm down," he said. "I don't know what is going on, but you're going to make yourself sick if you keep this up."

Trust Steven to come across as logical when she was flipping out. It only made her madder, furious really.

"Don't worry, it won't cost you a dime," she retorted. "Here, take this." She threw one of her sweaters into his arms so she could carry more and surprise him enough that she could escape the close confines of the closet. She couldn't breathe with him so close.

"I knew it," he said, following her into the bedroom but not relinquishing the sweater. Oh, well, she could get another one—after she found a *job*.

"You knew what?" she prompted, stuffing the already full suitcase.

"You've lost your mind. It was only a matter of time." He nonchalantly sat on the arm of one of the club chairs that flanked the fireplace. "I'm surprised you lasted this long."

Flummoxed, she quit fighting the zipper on the case and sank onto the bed. "I have no idea what you are talking about." She tiredly rubbed her brow.

"Ha," he said, tossing the sweater onto the seat. "Now you know how I feel." He sighed, his gaze softening as he watched her. "Do you think we could have an adult conversation? You tell me why you're angry and I'll tell you how stupid I was to say what I said out in the car, I didn't mean it the way it came out."

She pulled a tissue from the box on the bedside table, cleaned herself up, and met his warm gaze. "I'm such a mess."

He shook his head, rose, and joined her on the side of the bed after shoving the case out of the way. "You could never look bad to me, I love you." He put an arm around her shoulders and tugged her against his chest.

She closed her eyes and breathed in his woodsy-spice scent. Her husband. "I saw you with a woman," she whispered. "At the Drunken Lantern."

He stiffened, but instead of pushing her away, he pulled her closer. "Is that what this is about?" His voice rumbled against her ear. His hand under her chin tipped her head so she could look into his eyes. "That woman was a client. Her husband is leaving her and threatening full custody of their children. I was meeting with her to suggest marital counseling before the court steps in. Naturally, she was upset." He kissed her damp eyelids. "I would never cheat on you, baby. Do you believe me?"

Could she? His explanation rang true. She had a feeling she'd overreacted. Maybe her own insecurities had played tricks on her. Now, as well as saving her marriage, she needed to salve her guilty conscience and make reparations with her sister.

But for now, she had to make up with her husband. She lifted her lips and placed them against his mouth. "Kiss me."

CHAPTER

TWENTY-THREE

After three days, Holly was allowed to go home from the hospital with a stern warning from the doctor to take better care of her health.

She was waiting in the compulsory wheelchair when Levi arrived at the door to her room. Self-conscious, she tried to flatten her messy hair, then gave it up as a lost cause. "Sorry about this," she patted the arm of the chair, "the nurse insisted."

He smiled, eyes warm, then gathered the bag with her few toiletries and stopped to plant a kiss on her mouth. "Let's get you out of here before they change their mind; it's Christmas Eve."

Bemused, Holly put quivering fingers to her lips to hold the imprint of his touch as long as she could. The long white hall with a multitude of door-ways passed by in a blur, then they were passing the nurse's station decked out in poinsettias and holiday cards. A quick ride on an elevator with two other passengers, a woman with a pale, big-eyed child, no more than three and obviously battling cancer—another shorter, busier hall and then they were free.

Just as they left the protective overhang, a fine drizzle began to fall, but Holly didn't mind. It felt refreshing after being cooped up for days. Levi hurried them along though, bumping and bouncing over the rough sidewalk blocks until she laughingly told him to slow down. "My teeth are clattering."

He obeyed, but only after insisting she take his jacket as a makeshift umbrella. "Of course, the only parking space was at the far end of the lot. Keep covered, we don't want you to catch a cold."

"What about you?" she asked, peering from under the jacket to see him shaking his head like a wet puppy. An extremely handsome wet puppy.

He grinned at her. "It would take more than a little west coast rain to bring me down." He swerved around a van backing out of a stall and came to a halt by the convertible. "Your chariot awaits, Miss."

Holly giggled. "What are you so happy about?"

He came around, crouched in front of her chair, and took her hands. "Have you talked to your sister?"

She stared at the raindrops glittering on his eyelashes, her pulse thrumming. "No, why?"

He squeezed her fingers and she gathered strength for whatever he was about to say.

"She and Steven have sorted out their differences. They're together again. Just in time for Christmas."

Overjoyed, Holly threw herself into Levi's arms, then gasped when he overbalanced and landed on his butt on the wet pavement. "Oh no, I'm so sorry."

"I'm not." He stared at her and what she saw in his eyes made her heart stutter. Mortified, she tried to scramble out of his lap, then froze when her hand landed high on a muscular thigh.

"Levi—"

He closed his hand over hers to hold it in place and murmured, "Shh..."

His eyes darkened to cobalt and then his lips were on hers with gentle pressure. He tasted of coffee and mint; his mouth firm, yet tender. He coaxed her mouth open and their tongues flirted, entwining, withdrawing, then coming together again in a dance that grew more and more passionate.

Caught off guard, she broke away, stunned by the hint of vulnerability she caught in his eyes. "Levi, I..."

He shook his head and that sensual mouth quirked. "Way to knock a guy off his feet, Holly Tremaine."

"Can I help you there, Miss?" A man stood behind the wheelchair and stared down at them.

"Thanks, but I've got her," Levi answered, his gaze meshing with hers.

Holly flushed under the intensity of his expression. What was he suggesting? Did he...?

"Quit thinking so hard," he murmured as the would-be rescuer carried on his way. "I like you, Holly. A lot. We get along well—when you aren't trying to do me in—" He glanced meaningfully at her hand on his leg. "And I want to give us a try. What do you say?"

Holly didn't believe in miracles, but the sensations coursing through her veins couldn't be ignored. A long time ago, Steven had bruised her heart and Levi had been there to pick up the pieces. If she were honest with herself, he'd been there, in her heart, ever since.

She looked up as a bright ray of sunshine broke through the clouds and a rainbow appeared over the city. Life was about experiences; growing and changing was part of the process. She wasn't the person she'd been all those years ago. Innocence had given way to wisdom, and spontaneity to wariness. But that didn't mean she wanted to give up a chance for happiness.

She had a feeling Levi was that chance.

She looked at him and a smile broke across her lips. "I say what took you so long?"

TWENTY-FOUR

It was mid-afternoon before Holly and Levi arrived at her parents' home. Levi had to stop by his hotel to change after his encounter with the road, and then they'd done a quick shopping trip to pick up a few last-minute gifts for the children. The colorful lights, sparkly trees, and holiday music all combined to fill her with joy. The handsome man holding her hand as though he couldn't bear to let go... he made her heart smile.

The mouthwatering aromas of turkey, sage and rosemary hit them the moment they opened the door. Coats, boots, mitts and scarves led them down the hall like breadcrumbs to the den where Amy and Jacob were helping their dad decorate a massive seven-foot pine in an array of gold and silver ornaments.

Steven twisted at their entry, a string of lights

dangling between his fingers. He took in Levi's arm around Holly's waist and grinned. "I knew it," he crowed. "Aunty Holly has a boyfriend."

The kids jumped up and ran over, Amy trailing a length of garland she wore like a sash. "You're here. You're here." She grabbed Holly's hand and tugged. "Come help us make the tree pretty. Daddy said the presents can't go under until we're done." She pouted at her father.

"Actually, I said there might not *be* any presents if we don't get this finished," Steven corrected.

"Well, we can't have that," Levi said, lifting the bag full of gaily wrapped gifts he'd carried in from the car. "I didn't save my receipts; how am I going to return these?"

"Uncle..." Jacob rolled his eyes. "We know you're kidding."

Levi grinned, dropped the bag, and snatched his nephew into the air. "You do, huh? That's it, someone is getting socks and underwear for Christmas."

Amy giggled. "Not me, I don't want *underwear*."

"You're both getting coal if you don't get to work," Steven warned as he draped the lights around the top of the tree.

Holly laughed. "Sounds as though you have everything under control, so I'll go and see if they need help with dinner." She looked at Steven. "Where is Susan?"

He waved a hand toward the kitchen. "Helping

your mother, I think." Then, he turned to meet her gaze. "Glad you made it."

Her throat tightened. "Me, too." The tumultuous history between them had transformed into affection and for that she was grateful.

Levi caught her on the way out of the door. "Are you okay?" he asked, his brow furrowed. "Did we overdo the shopping?"

She shook her head and planted a kiss on his freshly shaved jaw. "I'm fine, quit worrying."

He leaned in close to her ear. "You'll have to wait until later to see your gift, I have something special planned."

Her pulse leaped, the sheer charisma of the man turning her deaf with want. "Hmm?"

He smiled, awareness flashing in his eyes. "Later," he repeated, and then he was gone, joining his brother stringing lights.

The sweetness of the scene stole her breath. It had been a long time since she'd looked forward to Christmas, but she was this year. Or she would be after she spoke to her sister.

She fingered the charm in her coat pocket as she made her way down the hall. Maybe Susan wouldn't even remember when they'd bought them with their allowance money, but it mattered to her.

Her mother and father were sitting at the table

with steaming cups of tea when she walked into the kitchen—and they were holding hands.

Holly smiled. "Does that mean what I think it means?"

Her mother's cheeks turned red, but she didn't let go. "Your father and I have talked. We're going to see a counsellor, and then we're taking a holiday. We've always wanted to visit Italy, maybe even renew our vows."

"Oh, Mom," Holly cried, rushing over to give them a group hug, fusing their hearts into one beating pulse. Family.

Her mother allowed it for longer than expected, then she shrugged free and rose. "Well, time to start the potatoes. Go find your sister, Holly. She makes the best gravy."

Blinking back happy tears, Holly headed down to the bedrooms and found Susan sitting on her bed.

She jumped up when Holly entered the room and swiped at moist cheeks. "I wasn't snooping," she said, her posture defensive. "I just..."

Holly closed the door and walked straight across to pull her sister into a hug infused with all the emotion she'd been too selfish to share over the years. "Merry Christmas," she whispered.

Susan grabbed on and squeezed the air from her lungs, but Holly didn't care. They were healing, she could feel it. So many memories passed wordlessly between them, good and bad. All of it binding together to make them stronger; resilient.

When they finally broke apart, Holly held out the silver heart charm, half of which was missing in a jagged line down the center. "Remember this?"

Susan's eyes widened. Slowly she tugged the chain around her neck out of her sweater to reveal the other half of the keepsake. "I've never taken it off, we made a pact."

Holly's eyes teared up again. "Sisters forever," she agreed.

Misunderstandings had torn them apart, but that was over now. It was never too late for the gift of forgiveness.

LATER, Holly cuddled on Levi's lap while he sat in a club chair. The room was dark except for the multi-color lights blinking on the tree and glinting off the ornaments. Presents were stacked hodge-podge under the pine and halfway out into the room. It had been hard to get the kids to sleep until their parents warned them Santa only visited the good kids on Christmas Eve. But now the house had settled for the night and they were taking advantage of the quiet to enjoy the newfound closeness between them.

"This is nice," she murmured, nuzzling his neck

and smiling at his involuntary shiver. "I'm going to miss it when I go back to New York."

Levi's languorous caresses stilled. "You're leaving?" He stood—dumping her in the chair—to stride across the room, the tree halting his progress. "When?"

Confused, Holly stared at his stiff back. "Probably after the new year, I have..."

Okay, fine," he interrupted, his voice brisk. "I'd better get going, tomorrow's going to be a big day." He glanced over his shoulder at her, his expression bleak under the blinking lights. "Goodnight, Holly." He walked out and a few seconds later, she heard the outer door close.

"What just happened?" she whispered. The warmth and intimacy of the past hour was gone, leaving an empty room behind. He'd been hurt and angry, she'd felt it emanating off of him, but why?

Then it dawned on her; he thought she was leaving for good.

She ran through the house and out the front door, heedless of the winter temperature. Levi had started the convertible and was waiting for the windows to clear. Holly raced across the cold, wet grass in her stocking feet and banged on the passenger side, begging him to unlock the door.

He reached across and opened the door, waiting until she climbed inside to give her hell. "What were you thinking? You just got out of the hospital. Are you *trying* to make yourself sick again?"

She shivered and wrapped her arms around herself to preserve heat. "Will that keep you from running away?" she stuttered.

Levi looked at her like she was crazy—and maybe she was—before peeling out of his coat to cover it over her from head to knee, and turn up the vents, though the still cool air blowing through them made her teeth chatter.

"I'm not the one who likes to pull disappearing acts. I'll leave that dubious honor to you," he muttered.

Well, she deserved that. Didn't have to like it though. "If you would have let me finish what I had to say, you would have learned that I plan on moving back to Victoria, but I need to sublet my flat, pack, and give notice with my boss, first."

He stared at her and a slow smile lit his face. "So, you're not leaving." He said it as a statement. "My bad."

Still miffed, she refused to be mollified so easily. "I'm not the same person who ran away from her problems, Levi. That girl didn't stand up for herself. I've grown up since then." She lifted her wet foot. "Enough that I chased through rain-slick grass in order to set things straight with a stubborn, hard-headed, wonderful man I've fallen in love with. Does that count?"

He took her face in his hands, the heat in his eyes doing more to warm her than a blazing fire. "Do you mean it?" he demanded.

"That you're stubborn?" she teased, then sobered. "Yes, I love you, Levi Anderson. I think it began the night of my sister's wedding. You took care of me then, and you've watched out for me ever since. I want to build a new life here, with you, if you'll give me a chance."

He leaned in and gave her a kiss that curled her toes. "I thought you'd never ask."

EPILOGUE

ight months later,

E A crowd of well over a hundred gathered for the ribbon cutting on the new Garden City Dance and Music Studio. Holly stared out at the faces of their potential new clients and a frisson of excitement tickled her spine. It was happening. She and her sister were officially in business together.

Susan hefted an oversized pair of red scissors in the air and shouted, "Ready? On the count of three."

Holly glanced over her shoulder and shared a giddy smile with their parents, Steven and Levi. She waved the kids forward. "C'mon, you two. You can hold the ribbon."

Jacob joined his mother and she showed him what to do while Holly helped Amy. "Okay, help us count," Holly called.

"Three."

"Two."

"One."

Susan snipped and the crowd cheered, surging forward to enter the newly refurbished warehouse on the bank of the Gorge. The giant space had been converted into three large studios; two for dance with floor-to-ceiling mirrors to reflect the students and the waterfront view beyond the windows; the other soundproofed and outfitted with everything from a baby grand piano to cellos, violins, brass instruments and a high-tech audio recording system for playback and rentals.

Susan was ecstatic, her life had a new purpose and she and Steven were expecting their third child. For Holly's part she'd privately feared giving up her professional career would leave her dissatisfied, but that hadn't happened. The thought of instilling her love of music onto a new generation of would-be concerto soloists carried its own thrill.

Levi had kept his agency in Vancouver, at least for now, but he did most of his work remotely and the studio was set up for his needs. Holly hoped one day soon he'd completely relocate. Eight months and things had never been better between them. They'd taken a big step and moved in together a couple of months ago and now she couldn't imagine waking up without him by her side.

Her parents had finally booked their trip to Rome and her father planned to ask her mother to marry him again at the base of Trevi Fountain. Holly made him promise to get pictures.

Needing a moment to recoup from all the excitement, she entered her studio and quietly closed the door. Her sister could hold down the fort for now. She ran her hand over the smooth lacquered finish on the piano, but her gaze was on the violin stand in the corner. The instrument drew her like a lodestone. The *Cecillio* made from solid maple and the bow with its Mongolian horsehair and ebony frog had seen her through many wonderful performances and now it would be used to teach others. The realization was bittersweet.

She turned as the door opened, ready to paste a social smile on for an interested parent or student but, instead, it was Levi who entered.

"Hey," he said, crossing to her side. "Everything okay?"

She nodded. "Just a little overwhelmed, I guess."

He drew her into his arms and kissed her brow. "That's to be expected. This is a big day. I'm so proud of you."

Her throat tightened. "Thanks to you and Steven. We couldn't have done it without you."

He grinned. "Who'd have thought we could handle a hammer without destroying what we touch."

She smiled. "You don't give yourself enough credit. Truly, Levi, I appreciate everything you did. I love you." She tightened her hold on his waist and leaned a cheek against his chest, comforted by the steady thump of his heart.

They stood that way for a few precious moments and then Levi stepped back, and the intensity of his gaze made her pulse jump. He reached into his pocket and came out with a small blue box—*oh, my God*— before going down on one knee.

"I wanted a special occasion, but now I realize this is the perfect time." He took her trembling fingers in his shaky hand and stared up at her face. "Holly Tremaine, I love your beautiful smile, how you care about others more than yourself, the scent of your skin, the way you feel in my arms—everything about you." He took a stunning solitaire and slid it onto her ring finger. "I want to build a life with you, have children and grow old together. Will you marry me?"

Holly could barely focus for the tears streaming down her cheeks, but she didn't have to see his beloved face to recognize him. He was her other half. "Yes," she cried, and threw herself into his waiting arms. "Oh, yes."

AFTERWORD

Reviews are the lifeblood of any successful author. Without you, we can't be heard.

If you enjoy the story, please consider sharing on your favorite social media sites, as well as GoodReads and from wherever you've bought the book.

Thank you,

Jacquie Biggar

Jacqbiggar.com

PREVIEW SKATING ON THIN ICE

Mac Wanowski was having the best night of his hockey career. Two goals and three assists with a period and a half to go. Everything was going their way. He should be a shoo-in for MVP. The Victoria WarHawks were playing on home turf to a full stadium of rowdy fans with fast ice—nothing could stop him now.

The blow came out of nowhere.

One minute he was flying down the ice with the puck held in the sweet spot of his stick, the crowd roaring his name, the net in sight, in the next instant Mac was shoved from behind and smacked into the boards. He bounced and went down hard on his right knee. The pain was immediate and intense. It sucked the breath from his lungs and left him seeing stars. He dropped his head between his arms and tried to remain conscious until the medics arrived. It was small consolation the refs caught the illegal move and rang the penalty buzzer.

Fricking Murtagh.

The other team's enforcer liked to pull sneak attacks. He'd done it before. Mac rolled onto his back and blinked as the auditorium swam before his eyes.

"Wow, man, that had to hurt." Samson chortled, skidding to a stop against the boards. The plexi-glass shook with the collision.

Edwards, the team's doctor skated across the ice in his dress shoes and dropped to his side. "Hey, Hammer, nice hit. How you doing?"

"Been better," Mac grumbled. He squinted through

the face-shield and yanked off his gloves. "It's the knee, Doc. Screwed it good this time." The helmet came next, clattering onto the ice along with his dreams.

"Don't worry. He will pay." Lazlo, the grinder, towered over Mac glaring at the other team as though daring them to come near.

"Keep it clean, boys," the ref said, gliding up to pat the Croatian's arm. "I don't wanna send you to the bench, but I will." He exchanged a look with the doc, then blew his whistle and waved an arm over his head. "Gurney's on the way."

Mac growled and tried to sit up, but Edwards forced him down. The guy might be old but working around a bunch of hockey players kept him in shape. "Take it easy, Mac. It's just a precaution. You don't want to aggravate that tendon any more than you need to."

Getting hauled off the ice like an invalid only added insult to injury. Not even the crowd's support could ease his wrath against the meathead who'd taken him down. He strained to see past the EMT's hold on the gurney. Murtagh sat in the penalty box, his arrogant gaze triumphant even as his coach tore him a new asshole from over his shoulder.

Pissed, Mac pointed and mouthed, "You're mine." Then they were in the hallway heading toward the dressing room and his adrenaline waned, leaving him drawn and listless. The knee throbbed, pressing uncomfortably against his protective padding. His shoulder ached from smashing into the wall and his insides jiggled like a bowl full of jelly. But if Doc gave him the go-ahead he could still make the third period. He needed to get out there and support his team, dammit.

Coach was waiting when he arrived, pacing and muttering while running a hand over his thinning pate. The second the EMTs set him down on the exam table Coach was breathing in his face.

"What the hell, Wanowski? I told you to pass! This superhero complex of yours is costing the team. Now what are we supposed to do, huh? We're already two men down and play-offs are coming up. Your actions tonight might have cost us the season. How do you feel now, asshole?"

Like shit, thanks for asking. The man had it in for him ever since Mac hooked up with his daughter for one never-to-be-repeated night, and nothing he did for the team was enough. It bothered him that this time Coach was right—he'd screwed up. Not that he could admit it, especially with all the interested ears wagging in the room. So, he said nothing.

The coach threw up his hands and stormed out of the room, heading back to what was left of the game. Mac just hoped they could retain their five-three lead until it ended.

"You like playing with fire, don't ya?" Doc Edwards shook his head. "Your contract is almost up with the WarHawks, Mac. Have you given any thought to what comes next?"

Mac frowned at the doc's back as he turned away to open his medical bag. "You hear something you want to tell me about?" He'd given three of his best years to this team. If the franchise planned to trade him off, the least they could do was tell him to his face.

Doc held up his hand. "Don't get your shorts in a knot, kid. I merely meant you can't play hockey forever. You must have a backup plan, right?'

Kid. Mac grunted as the other man loosened the ties on his knee guard. The resulting relief was quickly replaced by agony as blood rushed to the injury. He clenched his fists against the cool metal of the exam table and stared at the ceiling with its ugly track lighting while Doc poked and prodded the area like a sadist.

No, he didn't have a backup plan—this was it for him. Hockey was in his blood. It fed his dark soul and gave him the only true joy he'd ever known.

He couldn't leave the game.

"How bad, Doc?" He tipped his head to look down the length of his body and swore. Just as he'd thought, the knee was swollen and already showing signs of bruising. Last time he'd injured it, he'd ended up with water under the kneecap and had to have it drained. Fun times.

Edwards snapped an ice pack into action and set it against his skin before meeting his worried gaze. "I won't know for sure until we do x-rays. My best guess is your ACL." Mac winced. "Hopefully it's a sprain instead of a full tear which would mean surgery and months of rehab."

Christ, just what he didn't need right now. He laid down and covered his eyes with his forearm. "And if it's a sprain?"

"Sorry, Mac. You're still looking at two-to-four weeks recovery time, physio, and preferably crutches. I know someone, Sam Walters, who's good at this sort of injury. I'll call and see what I can get lined up."

Mac let him drone on with his voice of doom, meanwhile inside his stomach twisted into their own disastrous knots.

What was he going to do now?

Pick up your copy today!

MY GIFT TO YOU!

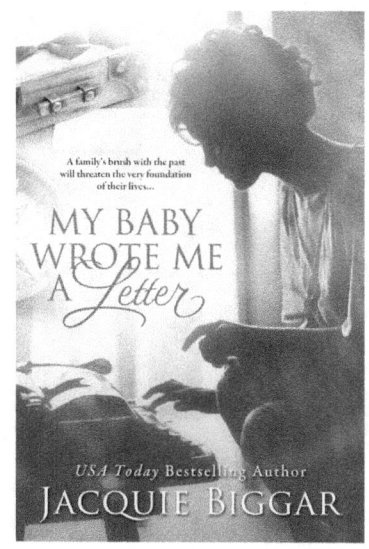

MY BABY WROTE ME A LETTER

A family's brush with the past will threaten the fabric of their lives.

Eight months pregnant and her Navy husband away on a mission, Grace Freeman craves the security of her childhood home in Canada.

When a letter written by her long-lost mother is found in an old writing desk it creates a tear in the fabric of her family.

Can Grace find a way to bring peace to those she loves, or will a message from the past destroy their future?

Newsletter subscribers also get bonus content and insider information every month. I love giveaways and there is lots of interesting stuff for me to share with you!

Newsletter- <u>Sign up Now!</u>

About the Author

JACQUIE BIGGAR is a USA Today bestselling author of Romantic Suspense who loves to write about tough, alpha males and strong, contemporary women willing to show their men that true power comes from love.

She is the author of the popular Wounded Hearts series and has just started a new series in paranormal suspense, Mended Souls.

She has been blessed with a long, happy marriage and enjoys writing romance novels that end with happily-ever-afters.

Jacquie lives in paradise along the west coast of Canada with her family and loves reading, writing, and flower gardening. She swears she can't function without coffee, preferably at the beach with her sweetheart. :)

Sign up now to keep up with Jacquie's new releases, excerpts, giveaways, and more:

Newsletter

jacqbiggar.com
jbiggar@jacqbiggar.com

facebook.com/jacqbiggar
twitter.com/jacqbiggar
instagram.com/jacqbiggar
amazon.com/author/jacquiebiggar
bookbub.com/authors/jacquie-biggar

ALSO BY JACQUIE BIGGAR

WOUNDED HEARTS SERIES

Tidal Falls

The Rebel's Redemption

Twilight's Encore

The Sheriff Meets His Match

Summer Lovin'

Wounded Hearts Box Set

Maggie's Revenge

With This Heart

The SEAL's Temptation

Secrets, Lies & Alibis

MENDED SOULS SERIES

The Guardian

The Beast Within

Virtually Gone

GAMBLING HEARTS

Hold 'Em

Crazy Little Thing Called Love

My Girl

Married to The Texan- Box set

BLUE HAVEN

Sweetheart Cove

Sunset Beach

MEN OF WARHAWKS

Skating on Thin Ice

The Player

THE DEFIANT SISTERS DUET

Letting Go

Finding Me

SINGLE TITLES

Silver Bells

The Lady Said No

My Baby Wrote Me A Letter

Tempted by Mr. Wrong

Valentine: A Hearts and Kisses Romance

Mistletoe Inn

The Sister Pact

Perfectly Imperfect

Love, Me